Sabonia

Sabonia

Nick Paratore

To order additional copies of this book, contact:
Xlibris
1-888-795-4274
www.Xlibris.com
Orders@Xlibris.com
814840

CHAPTER 1

The World's Balance

Space mirrors the oceans, mysterious in ways as the soul, which stands for all life in the universe. A commonality between us exists, in a spark of energy that guides us, leading us out of any abyss, one so deep within us it could never miss in the end. Whether we feel a light of sort along the way, one is there, one within our spirits.

A man, of the most noble, bearded, and of average height and decently charismatic looks, named Uljohn, has gone on longer he than ever has without a shave or shower. All he thought of was how to save humanity and how to save them from the brink of utter destruction, before it is too late. Even the wonders of the world itself were in jeopardy, the very miracles we have built with all the joy, pain, and hope imaginable, their homes, the great pyramids, and all of their favorite places to go.

All are being consumed in a way of such horrible violence that countless people simply do not know what to do, or where to hide from it, as it has spread everywhere they can imagine. At a time when spirits were believed to be as full of life as ever before, here stood earth, yet for how long or short was the question. Yet there walks a few heroes among them, some right under their noses, and others across great oceans. Each will surely be put to the test of our lives.

There has been a figure shrouded in the dark of shadows lurking. Although barely seen, he, or it, is often seen with only a few others. Rumored to come as a violent storms wind, always at night, under the moon's light. Whipping from out of nowhere, taking whatever life it chooses as a form of beast. With power enough to even entirely take over ones mind, sending them into a mental trance. Many have simply disappeared. Hence Uljohn's under managed appearance.

Standing by a window, partially braced by his arms, for his knees ache, Uljohn looks out over his home. The giant City of York, populated by millions. Hundreds of thousands less since chaos broke out. He felt humanities weight on his shoulders. Looking away from the sunset, he lowers his head.

The soothing thought of a fairly young, strong spirited like no other, named Willa enters his mind than. "Our last hope lie solely on my instincts." He says to himself. A long beat passes as a knock at the door uplifts him, raising his head. "Willa?!" He asks while opening the door wide. "There's no time, you were right Uljohn." Uljohn is shocked for a moment, frozen in time. He looks up to her, straightening up his posture, as well as his spirit.

He asks, "You mean, you feel it's true?" With the most hopeful eyes imaginable he looks to her, standing near the doorway. Realizing something vital to the world at large he waves her further into the room than shuts, and locks the door. "You were, I, I saw much. I can't explain it yet I have felt more alive than ever, as if things are connecting to me, things, in nature, from the stars."

Smiling, though awkwardly as he understands the hope he has could be less than one percent of a chance. Yet if that means peace, he will cross the ocean a thousand times. "That means I was right about..." Uljohn steps toward her comfortingly as she looks to him. "...Another, like you." He says at last. "Please Willa, you must remain hidden here while I find him." She hesitates than nods to him. He is about to turn, pauses, whispering, "Your family, does anyone know?"

Her reply comes in the firmest, softest manner, "I've told no one." So curious, she asks, how can you be sure there is another?" His reply comes as fast as anyone's sharpest instincts can ignite them to believe what there heart keeps reminding them of. "Because the world is big, and the universe bigger, and I believe whoever, whatever created all of it, has given us a way to protect it."

Weighing on his mind is the war shadowing their once wider spread civilization. How it has been weaving in and out of his mind, affecting those he cares for. The morning sun seemed to correlate timing wise with him striking the realization of just how many hardships he will come across. Despite its majestic light it was fading dimmer as somber had most all of humanity become. The city of York was far from the only one threatened for it was truly the entire world struck.

For this plan though, it was the best he could spawn and was filled to the rim with ingredients of absolute danger. All the council had agreed. He could tell for he did in fact know them as well as they know themselves. In essence that was his gift, reading people.

Each of York's Council wrapped their heads around Uljohn's proposal, based solely on his pitch. Face to face they granted his requests. For they saw what was reflected from his heart, and prayed he was right, for all they knew depended upon it.

War came onto them as earth shattering hurricanes do. The council did what they could to get each and every ship builder to begin Uljohn's design. Time drifted in spurts as all revolved as it does, naturally with a twist of order and chaos in all regards...hence the balance of the universe in all its wonder, accompanied by mysteriousness.

The knock on his door was what he had been preparing for. He gathered his belongings and walked to the pier, only a few short city blocks away. He thinks, "Here we go. Move on with the speed so forth coming from a clear head. Let concentration mend your pains, focus guide you, forever more."

On par with all he had held most dear he heard the sound by the waters edge, pushing him exactly to where he was supposed to be, to where he belonged. With his mind set ready he climbed on board.

The splashing waves against the wooden bulkheads on port and starboard sides of the ship recalled a childhood song he grew up with. His spirits lifted as a kite to strong wind.

Minimal crew was aboard tending to keep the vessel sailing as fast as possible.

Here, now with the port behind he realized with every fiber of his being that he would find what he needed. Oceans seemed small, all of the worlds, when he compared it to what was at stake did as well.

Sure his people had experienced warfare, though nothing like this. This was different, alien in every way to him. Enough to shake up humanity, so many have already been lost. He held onto everyone he loves, in the after world or not, and prayed for all along the way of crossing the great ocean before them. To an unknown foreign coast they head. Yet he, Willa as well, believed there is someone there to help.

Music of his own filled the sky along with the spirits of the crew entire. Uljohn played the flute and it wasn't long before dolphins made themselves visible. With the sunset behind them, the crews' spirits were strong. There fears were put aside, for the moments that passed into the night at least. Soothing was the melody, and animals among them.

Uljohn found himself surpassing the night till the early morning when he fell asleep.

Soon, all around him was a nasty storm, rolling them over even, swells the size of mountains. After the days of drifting miraculously they pull up to the shores of a foreign, completely uncharted land and it felt like no other sensation. All the crew welcomed the site of dry land. Which was really the land of elves, dwarves, and the rare dwelven.

On his knees in his cabin Uljohn prays, for the darkness that has crept over the land to lose to the sun shinning bright. Forces unknown had been unleashed on this once peaceful globe. For all his hope, happiness and spirit spoke to any listening. A tear rolled now along his cheek, as he says the following aloud, "May it be the gods, us, or another way, yet please, to all those living and non I pray for better days, ones upon which we all can be as happy as can be.

On the other side of the ocean, there was a light yet still. One, who shares the strength of Willa, lies down on a fresh trimmed grass, ever growing under the blessings of a hot sun. His name is Sabian; he is an elf, a Sabonian elf, from the land called Sabonia. His ivory skin looks as the snow would. His culture, filled with civil war, is mixed between three skin tones, ivory, gray, and ebon, each earth like. He leans against his favorite tree. One of the nicest ink pens he's ever had is pressed against the page of his small maroon leather book. He begins writing the title; 'Treaty of Union' than continues writing.

Sabian thinks the following to himself, "If we did not judge by looks, we would find such strength in uniting, enough to survive…" he stops, thinking he hears something.

Snow falls on him from a half lively tree branch above. In this city, named Frondrok, snow is a fairly normal, yet what is not are traces of a world deteriorating. Despite the mess, he smiles to himself. Looking up while brushing off he notices the tree has split in two. That gave him a good feeling. He balances the book on his knee a moment, takes a deep breath than folds the book closed.

His city borders the northern ridge of the continent of Sabonia. Here, live Sabonian Elves, like humans, a brilliant, yet flawed species. Remarkably, an immensely fiery sun kept the local forest of pine trees flourishing. A forest where he, his family, and friends have had many an adventure. This soothes him like really no other thing. On this seemingly normal day, he starts to stand up when the unthinkable happens. He hears distant footsteps, and he had secretly wished it were the love of his life, yet he has not met her yet.

Another, of whom the likes he has never seen only imagined, a human, now with a slight limp and water logged head from his journey. Uljohn by himself comes out of the forest, heading toward Sabian. The others the human saviors' crew remained behind off the path as a precaution, for there is no need to scare off someone who they are coming to for aid. The sunlight makes it very difficult for Sabian to make out who is coming. "Who goes there?!" Sabian calls out, holding one of his hands up to block the light.

What he can make out thus far strikes his eyes, as an alien, noticing the person does not have pointed ears, yet is taller than most dwarves. "An ally, who needs help!" Uljohn replies, with desperation at the core of his tone. Sabian walks toward him exponentially more curious with each passing second.

Practically face- to- face- now, Sabian asks, "My help?" While at that moment the sun at lasts is blocked and for the very first time in his life Sabian meets a human being. The elf looks all around, a bit nervously, as if to- let someone else, anyone else, to see what he's seeing.

"Please, we need your help, every second counts. The world has never been more dire." Uljohn says, a small handful of steps closer, yet about ready to fall from exhaustion. Battered were his hands, half full of salt water was his stomach still yet he carried onward.

With utter amazement every bit of Sabian expresses his shock. Oddly speechless, Sabian finds himself hearing Uljohn, as he is captivated, led in a blur of listening to him going on and on. He finds himself on the human's stealthily ship, leaving his people to save another. By trusting in his heart, he is confident he has heard the truth.

Once there on the shores of The City of York, with the great ocean behind them at last Sabian and Uljohn took some sort of relief. As eyes fell on him pupils widened as they felt an allure transpiring from him that transcended to the core of this audience and well beyond to the distant elven lands he originated.

With all his heart he wished he had the strength to not be speechless when in that first state of awe when seeing Uljohn. Yet he just could not. For the first time in his life he never felt more like the granules on the shore guided out to sea by the waves swept away by the goings on. He didn't tell anyone, without so much as a note. Foolishly perhaps, though proud still, willing to do all he could, for anyone.

He was as unique to them as they were to him, as the hemisphere he comes from is a population of elves; as varied as the people around him now, bearded, short, fat, and skinny just like humanity. Many in York wanted to ask this and that, with both curiosity and fear even, while dwelling at the root was concern, for their very lives, and those they cared for.

A Council of three takes a single pace closer to Sabian, standing dumbfounded before them. Uljohn is a professor, a diplomat, and a townsman, who often voiced his opinion in a rather non- restraining way. For him what he had experienced in life there was not much anyone could push on him that would cause him more pain.

An elder of the church was to Uljohn's left. She was one of the closest and diehard representatives of the holy spirit much of the world believed in with all that comprised them. Much had changed at this point from the war striking their shores. Which is the reason why they stand before Sabian. Little did they realize they needed the one given the name Willa equally.

For she stood fiery, diplomatic like in a way, and to Uljohn's right. For she is a gifted person, who like Sabian, knew that everyone has some type of gift. The question is whether it will take a lifetime or not to discover what that gift is. Willa was not much more than half Uljohn's age, though numbers determine little, she is a prodigy among billions. A city terrorized of late by violence will certainly need to believe in all that which is good around them, as well as within.

"All of us need your help." Uljohn says. Uljohn was the only person with a pulse that knew Willa had this special gift like Sabian, The Magic of the Stars. He admitted to himself and to her alone that he had no idea how to get it out of her. Overriding that was his instincts that had carried him and his people thus far. Not even she knew. Soon they will find out that this gift is not only one of healing, though one that could do much harm, as the stars can.

Children so happy, so full of life, and so sadly ended in consequent in the recent months. Taken from this world from the vicious plot of Sorg and his underlings, from his secret army shadowing the world entire, humanity first. Sabian finally asks, "What am I doing here, and where exactly is here?"

The bringer of this evil is one from a different world, far from earth. His parents named him Sorg. No one knows that besides those within his army he explicitly trusts. He had had come in a tornado of an ambush, using violence to get what he wanted. Countless lives were lost, good people and innocent people taken only because this world stood divided. Cracking like an egg because of the many who had prejudices towards one another, whether from their skin color, or other indifferences. They were lost nearly in their own civil wars, their own hatred of those on the other side of borders.

Sorg, through the Black Lion, Diterexitre, and Cao Nikita, had begun the hostile take over of York a piece at a time. Manipulating the Sabonian elf named Diterexitre long ago, from the beginning, even before actually meeting him face to face. Yet at this point what allured Sorg further was how he suddenly sensed Willa's power much greater now, while near to this new player, Sabian.

Acting on those instincts, the alien dark lord nods to the lion and Cao. The twosome walks out of the dark labyrinth out into the night. Now the cat had felt what Sorg did. Unsure he was drawn, feeling the last shred of hope he seemed able to summon.

Some time later, "Peace, longing for this thing so close to your heart, so much that it dictates a craving, that it turns into a dream you desire day in and day out. Without desire what would we be? What would we have? As the world rotates in the manner that it does, we may be happier remembering we are all miracles, whether our dreams come true or not, they are a part of us. That should be more than enough, spread that to everyone in this city, if you want my help." Sabian says to Uljohn and Willa in the middle of the cities main square. All eyes of the city on them, as many are eavesdropping.

Night was settling entirely now as two figures kept in the shadows. Darkness acted as blankets for them, which was a common comfort for foot soldiers such as these. Cleverly this twosome were hand in hand, figuratively speaking. Cao Nikita, in the physical form of a woman, is a shape changer. The Black Lion, a fully- grown feline, are rumored throughout the city to be 'The Night Stalkers.' Nailed onto posts one can see a piece of beige paper with those same very words, 'Night Stalkers', followed by the word 'Beware.' Underneath. Small signs, for the sake of the children, never the less eerie warning that has sent chills up many a spine.

Overlooking Willa and Sabian, the Black Lion signaled for Cao to wait. Yet perplexed Cao did agreed. An inner instinct had been struck much as an uplifting cord would to a heavy, somber song. A glimmer of hope came to the lion. Fair morals that contrasted their masters circumvented, stemming from whom the lion watched.

The ensnared dark twosome caught wind of the words of a clothing shop- keeper, a baker, and a farmer who were walking below by the hilltop they were a top. "Best we be locking up and heading home for the night you know Olan." One said to the other. The farmer replies, "Do you believe in those Night Stalkers?" The threesome, for whatever the reason be, looked to Willa, Sabian, and Uljohn curiously. Uljohn was mid striding walking to others in the council standing in a circle nearby.

"Bravery leads to confidence." Says Sabian, glancing at them and then at Willa. They pause a moment than simply nod and continue walking slowly. "I believe that with every fiber of my being."

The somewhat tall, muscular, ivory skinned, black haired Sabian says that. Pleasantly, deep down recognizing a kindred spirit he's found in her, perhaps in Uljohn as well. Even the shop owners standing idly by on the corner, pretending they aren't listening to the rumored heroes of the city nodding to each other.

The Black Lion, Cao as well, wanted to know more about what they were overhearing from their vantage point. As every word sheds light on their otherwise dreary, suppressed lives there caught to a degree in mind control. A thing holding on by a thread, though a thing that even he, the lion, admits at most times is as small as a spark. All and all this was the lions' chance for freedom, his last chance. Whether or not Cao was moved the way he was was yet to be seen.

The wind escort's clouds aside, revealing a crescent moon, so beautifully carved as a masterpiece of mother natures. Well all and all as all things, good or bad, they evolved. For that was the very state of, well everything, by grand design. The end of anything is the path to a new beginning. If not for the cat's request to hold the attack Cao Nikita would have considered this a mission of complete normalcy, which would be attacking in the numerous ways they could to further their masters web. The lion, holding on by a thread, has already made the distinct connection that Sabian and Willa are the source he felt while beside his 'so called master earlier'.

This was lions' chance at freedom, and eight lives were past. Every fiber in his being resonated with that. Over the years he realized how short life is. What mattered in this moment was his decision. He made it, and in one swoop he nodded good- bye to Cao and walked out of the shadows to the other side and astonishingly breaking his master's will enough to embrace his ninth life.

Sabian and Willa were the only ounces' to notice the cat. Uljohn was addressing a group of worried villagers who were surrounding him by the dozen. No one seemed to even see the cat at all. Sabian and Willa put together that the dark side was among them stalking the feline.

Cao followed, strutting like a young, fairly cocky, princess, one foot in front of the other, bestowed with a portion of her master's deep fountain of magic, as well as beholder to her own quite special gifts. She lived on her own planet for a long time, comparatively speaking to years in human terms, before it had undergone a devastating war, one in which had tumbled towers, crumbled bridges, uprooted about everything the population held dear.

The promise of ever lasting life came from Sorg. This was what he promised to countless others. Like never before Sabian and Willa feel the conflict within the lion incrementally as he nears although Cao's is undetermined. A brief moment passes for the foursome as they exchange glances. Cao steps beside the lion, a handful of yards away from the two protectors at hand.

"Curious", Willa says, "Why does no one else see you?" The lion raises his head in order to reach out to Sabian and Willa as the following is heard as a reply. "A cloak, we are to recruit whoever we can, all for a terrible army. If the Dark Lord knew I was warning you, its…." Yet as the lion is about to continue he stops himself, feeling a twisting change in the wind, and the coming of his terrible, spiteful master.

Sabian and Willa tense up. Sabian takes a large, firm step toward the Black Lion and Cao Nikita.

The planet, sun and moon align in a certain way as consequent to both the feelings of the protectors adjusting to the rising conflict. Vast energies resonate on a universal scale connect with Willa and Sabian, in similar ways. While around the hills nearby the coast, a tornado grew, one that Sorg himself was in the center of. Children, adults, seniors alike were terrified, to the point of hearts pumping as though there may be no tomorrow. Now they hear the rumbles and whipping winds as if the elements are in agony.

"Find cover!!!" Sabian shouts at the top of his lungs, thinking not only of his people, his friends or family, though literally everyone as a brother or sister. Uljohn is running up from behind them with a trail of guards and diplomats. Villagers, spotting the tornado by the hundreds, soon tens of thousands, run and shriek for their loved ones.

Sorg and his assistants, in their separate displays of power, join in the onslaught, all except the Black Lion. Diterexitre came from out of nowhere, much to Sabian's utter shock, "Diterexitre, but how is he here?" Uljohn and Willa, standing now beside Sabian shake their heads, in disbelief themselves at the site. A roaring, flare of light around Cao and Ditereitre take shape, in purples and pinks.

Buildings fall as they are struck with the dark magic, feeding off of the populaces segregation and hatred virtually the same. Hearts break, with a multitude of screams death had come to many an innocent over this once grand coastal city thriving with good fortune.

The sun was about to rise. From the pure connection Sabian and Willa have with it, they communicated on some unknown level. Sabian erupted in light, all around his body. They were able to channel together. That's when it happened.

The good people of York and certainly well beyond realized they chose their guardians as well as could be. A blue, red, and white, hot ray of light shines out of Sabian and Willa's chest, striking Sorg, Cao, and Diterexitre, sparing the lion.

What a contrasting thing of nature it was that all those that bared witness to it would take the site with them forever more as truly the world's first world war. Shedding the evil light and such away, piercing hell itself, did the light of the Magic of The Stars. Sorg and his crew fled as quickly as they had approached. The people were shocked, in utter awe at the site.

Some had felt hope returning while others were lost in site of the dead round them. Sobbing bellowed in the background all the while the opposing forces of the world collided. Sabian and Willa had not given up, yet there victory came at a high cost.

Barely standing, the protectors collapse, for it was all they could do to stop the utter madness. Mothers, fathers, toddlers, even the local pets had come out of where they found shelter. Seeing more clearly at this point what in the world was transpiring.

Uljohn looked around for Willa. Calling her name, "Willa?!" He was stunned, shattered in almost entirety to see her lying as still as a rock beside Sabian, from the looks of it barely breathing. Petrified eyes looked onward, the council's as well as the innocents saved, worried that they lost those dearest to them from left to right. Uljphn kneels beside the fallen protectors, angels if you would, whispering to him-self, "Please be alright, please, I had no idea, please."

Precious to so many hearts were the churches, and favorite shops such as Franks' Bakery on Willet Street, on the corner of York's Main Square. Symbolic of their way of life, partially now obliterated. Even materialistic things such as that mean the world to some people. With sunrise on the brink the survivors were reminded that another day was before them. Thank the noblest, bravest soul gods for that. For the chance to rebuild, and heal from their many wounds and losses were here.

Calling upon the Council of York, letters were written, sent with great care to the wisest clerics across the known world. Scriptures were going out all over the continent especially. Although hardly the thing of elven magic, humanity had learned a trick or two over the ages. Enough so that Uljohn knew there was more to Willa and what he sensed from across the ocean in Sabian. Within the next days certain songs were sung in high hopes that certain ears, the right ears, and only the right ears, would hear them.

After all, there were monumental pyramids built in distant lands that Uljohn had read about in ancient texts. One point he would raise in the morning during the meeting was the strong possibility that the chamber of healing would answer their prayers. Though even he at this point was doubtful.

Uljohn and the Council of York, its reserve members and all searched on. The net of healing would now be cast. Standing for more than they ever have, in the most challenging of ways. For now there was no one else. Their hopes were so entrusted, embedded, into the ties they made with Willa and Sabian.

It was up to them, normal men and women, with no special magical powers. Uljohn felt he had to rise up to another level. He pushed himself before time and again over his life course. Yet this time all he truly needed was a bit of quiet to clear his head in order to strategize.

While in the dingy Dark Lord's cave of a lair, there were harsh repercussions being followed through on for betrayal, so silent he remained, born to be King of The Jungle, forced into slavery, he endured the torture Sorg inflicted on him as if he was answering his own need to become more than he ever was. Pain has an ironic way, whether physical or not, to reinforce the spirit in an uncanny, brilliant way.

The Black Lion held onto that thought as well as the face of Willa and Sabian standing before him not so long ago. The sound of their voices anchored him so, so near to freedom. From the innocence of their philosophy he knew they were somehow the key to his freedom from the prison he was in.

Before Sorg had assaulted him with a spell that had controlled much of his mind, he remembers catching a glance at one of the shops in the center square called Frank's Bakery. The three merchant owners crossed his mind after that, specifically the way they embraced togetherness. That feeling hadn't crossed his mind in quite some time. In truth it was so long ago that he was together with his family, as a mere cub. Nevertheless, he had found his anchor in this storm of pain his master had inflicted.

Cao Nikita remarkably was becoming more empathetic, to the extent that she contemplated even risking her self to free the lion. Yes, she admitted, there was a one percentile she would actually go for it, though still, for here this was a moral break through. She was magnetized to how courageous he was. How innocent too he was when she had observed Sorg's orchestration on the eve of his kid napping, or cat napping. Curled up snuggling away as he shared the warm, loving, embrace of his siblings and parents.

She was about to walk away from where she was overlooking the cat being tortured when Diterexitre appears. "What are you thinking?" Asks Diterexitre, he who was given his name by his parents, Lopah and Loran, two mysterious outlaws. Tragically they fell into the afterworld. If that was not enough for one to bear, he had endured watching them die.

In a sharp reply Cao Nikita says, "Why do you ask?" Diterexitre looks over to the lion. "I feel its obvious, you and the beast have been something of a pair. Have you, as he does, not have your doubts about our path?" Somewhat raspy, jaded, yet firm, his voice rumbles nerves within her.

With the entire guile she can summon her reply comes smooth, soft, "I have no doubt. Nor should you. I will serve our master to the end." Diterexitre raises an eyebrow than nods to her. Diterexitre found Sorg not too long ago, seemingly by accident, according to Sorg's explanation, thus far. For there was a day when Diterexitre walked in a slightly different light.

CHAPTER 2

A Change In The Wind

Walnut colored eyes, one named Alderon, who has ebon skin, and embroidered robes, from the land Sabian is from, has ebon skin hears the songs of Uljohn and the other humans. Although only a short time has passed since his disappearance he had an enormous feeling that he needed help. To warrant such a style of departure, without a note, a word, a hint, all seemed to point in the direction that foul play had to be at hand.

He seeped into the most profound state of meditation he has ever been in order to find his long, lost friend, attuned to the agonizing cry for help that the Black Lion had cast out. Next he truly felt what he was after, what the world, perhaps the entire universe needed. He found where Sabian was the one who was said to be the savior, bringing their entire planet from war to peace. So said elven ancients.

After he awoke he called upon Drusaka, the cleric of clerics around the area to say the least, as well as a good friend to Sabian. What became the priority was bringing him home. Everything depended on this. Alderon, finessing the winds and waters, was to summon the spirits of nature itself. Long ago his ancestors did the same, he found he could communicate to the elements as distant brothers or sisters could fishing within the gigantic, infinitely populated universe.

Rare as a fourleaf clover it was even from the beginning of time for one to even become a wizard. In truth, anyone could do this if they could reach deep enough within themselves, so said ancient texts. Concentrating hard enough, feeling as openly as they could, whether spirits that were close to one, or never knew though want to be remembered, one must reach out of their norm. Like simply moving is going through a state of change, every sense accumulates, absorbs what it picks up on. Our imagination standing either behind or in the front line with our senses receiving.

Hence we live, as we change, we grow in immeasurable ways. Even spiritually. Drusaka, who has ivory skin, and Alderon, both appearing in there forties to fifties, in similar garments of leather, wear cloaks of earth tones. Weight wise Drusaka out does Alderon as he has a big pot- belly that he wears well. Near the shores of the City of York, they attune their sharp senses best they can within the harsh environment. Never before have they flew so far, that did not stop them. They swallowed their fears swirling in fatigue.

Forcefully driving themselves harder they cut through the airways like a sharp knife through warm butter, reaching to each of their cores resisting best they can, working together best they can. Drusaka heals them as they make head- way, falling deeper into meditative state of consciousness.

At last a mile away from the coast they spot York City, what is still standing at least. They ready themselves. The mage falls into a semi conscious state to pinpoint all he had sensed earlier…The Black Cat their future King Sabian, and the cause of their pain.

The only clue is that he sensed a unique type of energy among the others like a final piece to a puzzle of salvation, one he had never felt before or heard of. He could only gather this was from somewhere distant, or if his mentor, in all of her wisdom and age had. They crossed the ocean, the plan was to set fire to this darkness they felt. So that is exactly what they did. Only barely able to stand, Alderon was exhausted.

Yet he looks up to Drusaka, "You have healed me this far, my friend, though this next spell will certainly tire me out, for how long I know not". They look to each other for a moment, sharing a friendship, than Alderon goes under a spell. "I will do all I can." Drusaka says, breathing deeply the shore air round them.

Within the dark lair smoke was accompanied by a crackling noise in the back- ground. Shockingly to all those who lived there a massive fire erupted. The lot of them had set aside their personnel dilemmas for the meantime, for even death dealers, death had come to knock at their door. One way or the other, they had to answer that.

Sorg had set the cat in glowing black, purple, and pink chains, than was off. "Who started the fire?!" He asked himself. He locates first Diterexitre, than Cao Nikita. After that he pauses for a second, thinks hard than decides to give the Black Lion one more chance, yet to his astonishment when he returns he finds he is not there. The chains, thought to be ever lasting, forged from his ancestors, from his home world, laid shattered. Sorg shouts out in anger. "No!"

Changes were taking place to no end. Here and there, all over the world, within everyone, and everything alive, with time, a friend that brings us to where we need to go. Balancing all that there is. One comforting thought is that there is a cycle to life in that it is a chain, not that binds us as straps though one that binds us together. Each link independent in itself, as mighty as a star, yet not much without the others beside it.

Back on the beach, Drusaka holds his friend up as he falls in and out of consciousness, "Hang on Alderon, and stay with me!" Drusaka shouts. While not too far away the Black Lion took the fire as a sign from whatever god or goddess could exist out there. He followed the sound of Alderon's struggling; whispering level voice is heard inside his head, "Strive on, as the tides to the shore rid away, bringing something new entire."

The lion does just that, courageously reaching above his aching body. Purely his spirit drives his body onward. Once at the shore the lion is taken up in the winds of the wizard. Headway is steadily made to the city of York. To the astonishment of the city they witness the most spectacular sight of the threesome nearing on foot. Drusaka, doing all he can to partially hold Alderon up with his decently shaped shoulder. Yet contrasting those people there were those that were fearful.

Distant screams, even battle cries shrieked out as the wizard, lion, and cleric neared. Despite hammering and such by the hands of the construction rebuilding their city everyone's attention was drawn. There were those who even ran into hiding, not waiting to see if these were angels or arch- angels. "Run! Hide!" A countless voice cried out.

Many were drawn to a flashback of when Sorg had attacked. After all no one in their society had such power. Willa, unconscious still knew not what she could do, that day she and Sabian saved the city, quite possibly billions, was a surprise indeed. In the back of her mind she wondered if Uljohn knew what was going to happen that night. Yet she still, as Sabian, lie motionless in the chamber of healing.

Uljohn's attention, as countless others, had been grabbed by the new comers arrival. Alongside other council members, he ran toward where he saw them landing. Guardsman, soldiers, of every thinkable assortment flocked over to the scene stirring the city entire. The two Sabonians picked up that Uljohn and many others were surprised yes, but not to see their kind.

Alderon breaks the ice, making a peaceful introduction when he is within earshot, "I'm Alderon, friend to Sabian." With every word he speaks he is surrounded by a growing number of citizens.

"Why is this beast with you?" Says Uljohn. Alderon chooses his words wisely, making his point brief as possible. "We have questions of our own, yet the beast means well. His conflict, which side to belong, is what led us here." Many, at least in the nearby vicinity relax to a major degree as Alderon's words soak into them. That combined with Drusaka's calming spell casted with the upmost discreetness.

The wolves, dogs, and such farm animals of the city are going ballistic over the Black Lions' presence. "Please, time is crucial more than ever. Would you lead us to Sabian? We are here to help, all of you." Drusaka adds.

CHAPTER 3

Here in the council's newly designed healing chamber all who cared got to work. Their purpose, do whatever they could to save Willa and Sabian. Some were the 'push up their sleeves' type, while others were the 'polish their glasses type…few were both. All and all Drusaka took charge as an experienced captain rolling with everything he had and not what he did not.

The cleric hoped he could live up to their expectations, to the world for that matter. Cleric or not he could not admit in front of the others he was baffled to a degree as to the severity of the root of Sabian's illness. Perplexingly so on a good note, one of the best notes society has had of late. Willa was slowly bouncing back before his eyes. What made it more odd was he who is of his own kind wasn't responding to his remedies, yet the one from a foreign land was.

Healing as Drusaka explained to all of who comprised the council was as fine as a science as it gets. Unknown to most were the true complexities involved of the body, mind, and spirit. How they are connected as one, to one another, as well as how they are connected to the outside world.

Drusaka locked himself in a small area surrounded by not much other than a jug of water scroll, ink, a feathered pen, and each of which times two. After the good news of Willa he was harder on himself. Shutting out all he could, even a breeze filled with fresh air. Asking to not be bothered with anything at all under the sun, including the illnesses that were plaguing the city such as the black ooze. An oil, jelly like ooze that the dark ones had casted wherever they could, one that aided their dark spells, for they suspected as much.

Thankfully the town was far happier that one of their own had recovered. A new thought dawned onto the cleric, possibly the answer. He was writing do's and do not's based on his current knowledge and the beliefs of those he had studied when he began to write so fast that his pen snapped.

At the same second a tapping at the door struck. "Drusaka, it's me Alderon!" In a flashing scurry for the door he jumped out of his crude though effective chair. Banging his knee on the way up, grunting to himself. "I've got it!" Drusaka shouted, bracing his knee with one hand and answering the door with the other.

"You alright?!" Alderon takes notice to him holding his knee then saddening, the cleric looks away back to his desk.

"What's wrong?" The woozy Alderon asks while Drusaka limps aside, making room for Alderon to enter the small room. Aware further and further with every second that passes of exactly how deep the wound in Sabian must be.

Drusaka than looks down to the ground around the same time Alderon fixes his eyes on him. "Drusaka, tell me, any luck?" Drusaka looks down to the scroll. Alderon, "I do not need to remind you of how important this…"

Jumping in, Drusaka surprises Alderon, "Something otherworldly!" Drusaka is about to spit out the rest of his thoughts when Alderon inquires, "Other worldly?" "Meaning there is no other way I know to cure him. I am, I am out of ideas!" Drusaka replies.

"Forgive me." Drusaka says lowly. "There is nothing to forgive my friend. Together, we will find a way." Alderon replies kindly. "I'm not sure you understand." Drusaka limps over to his chair and sits down, starring off. "This is like nothing anyone has encountered." Drusaka says.

Alderon, "We will take him back to Sabonia and have every …" Drusaka interrupts, "You don't get it Alderon! If I can't find a cure for him the chances of someone else finding one do not exist!"

Alderon takes a long moment, choosing his next words ever so wisely, "I would not have brought you here if I did not think you are the best…though its friends and family perhaps could do what no one else could." Alderon keeps his calm as best he can, as well as his hopeful attitude about him.

Drusaka sighs, "You have a point." They take a moment, now looking each other eye to eye, "So tell me, any theories at all, no matter how far fetched?" Drusaka slowly though surely rises from his seat and says softly, "Well, there is one. Long shot at best. Come with me."

The two of them enter the healing chamber where Sabian is inside, "Please, leave us." Drusaka states, than nodding to each of the servants, nurses, and other clerics as they leave the room. "I've been the one who keeps fearing the worst, even before you said what you've said." Says Drusaka.

"Now you wanted theories, no matter how outlandish. If you're truly ready, you may want to brace yourself." Drusaka states. "Go on." Alderon does his absolute best to seal up any fear he has. He has, as Drusaka, come a long, long way.

"Something has been planted in him." Drusaka falls silent, observing his friends next expression. "As if something, perhaps alive is in him?" Alderon draws a blank, asking away.

"Yes, acting through him." Drusaka says in return. Alderon than continues, "You should know, that I understand you feel like you have not done what I, what Sabian's other friends and family have asked, both of us to do, yet I believe that only you could have gotten us this far."

Sometime later that evening under the brilliant luminance of a full moon. Others are drawn to the healing chamber, others who care much for what is going on. Willa and Uljohn walk into the room. The escort closes the door Drusaka leans over to him and asks, "Would you please have the lion brought in here?"

Drusaka turns to the others, "Whatever this is, and it has the counter intelligence to go against my every move. That is why we have asked for all of you here. Together, god willing, we will be enough."

Long moments pass as they exchange glances, each following Drusaka's every guiding measure and resolve. With all their hopes tied into one purpose. A general request for aid anyone can offer goes out to the people near and abroad. One of hope, to convey the urgency, for the world did depend on it. Without delay they begin the next step, as time is of the essence, they listen to Drusaka's every word with the upmost attentiveness. Repeating what he chants… "Alin- Goth-Val", repeated again and again.

"Close your eyes, you as well." Drusaka looks to each of them. The lion standing there attunes to every animal it has ever known. Spiritually reaching to their hearts in a plea to connect with a kindred spirit. The combined efforts of the group create the walls to shake. A blue energy illuminates the room than, flashing brighter and brighter.

Drusaka opens his eyes to check on his patient than the group, noticing some of their concentration and strength wavering, "Concentrate!" He shouts. The group tightens up their posture, paralleling their focus on the task at hand.

Too late to avoid the other side of this world however, evil has begun to sick its talons in once more. Beginning with an eerie sound, nearly indescribable, as a twisted wind, desperately clawing into where it is unwanted. Screaming rooted from a source as vague as the sky itself.

One who has ever heard the whirlwinds of a cyclone or tornado can feel what the five some felt pierce their ears. Swirling black, pink, and purple energy enters the chamber, seeping in from all sides around the doors as a violent force.

They begin shaking at the knees, drenched in sweat, and on the verge of collapsing from their efforts. Resilient, the Black Lion remains solid in posture, grunting away…taking a place of leadership in order to finish what they began. The lion in all his sureness, wrapped within his sharp instincts senses the dragon Graziloth, dwelling inside Sabian.

One who can become the tiniest dragon or biggest within the known universe, a title so very few even know of, in all existence. A sinister purpose no doubt brews from the blackened heart of Sorg. The non- admitting weary Alderon does all he can to help Drusaka heal Sabian. He feels twin energy to the one he'd picked up on all the way from the other side of the ocean. He and the others hear a creaking and cracking sound as the main door begins to give way.

Moments later it does and a small astral dragon rises' out of Sabian's body. Drusaka connects with the others, waving his hands over his head. Sabian, than hovers. "Now lion!" Drusaka shouts. The lion blinks to Drusaka than lets out a terrifying roar that sends Graziloth, in all of his pink scaly body, out of Sabian's chest. The dragon like beast though winded, moans in pain, than growling as it begins reentering Sabian. Just than Willa's eyes open wide, she, staggering to stand, painfully raises her hands.

The Magic Of The Stars comes streaming out of her finger- tips, in a blue, red, and white stream of light all of which bombards Graziloth. The beast, in a partial astral and solid form, screams out in tremendous agony than simply fades away into the air, leaving behind an ear-piercing roar of its own. One that rocks the very ground, shaking the chamber and directing it right over Sabian. Sabian's eyes open. All of the others sigh in relief.

CHAPTER 4

Sorg, yet still beside himself thinking this and that and the other thing, began to concentrate at last. Getting what he pushed for, as he was accustomed to do since being left alone as a child in the middle of a frightening place. He was sculpting his mind to what had happened, the fire, losing the lion, than the cherry on top was sensing even though subtle...there was a conflict raising within Diterexitre and even Cao Nikita.

This gave him pause, which the dark master of the mystic arts had not been use to in some time. A new resistance stemming from these newly found heroes. Thousands already had fallen, at least the accountable, yet he would never give up. Crossing an ocean to save one of their own, setting a blaze to his lair, escaping, healing, and even manipulating the lion to help heal the one he overheard was named... Sabian.

The elves certainly created walls for Sorg. He regrouped with every step he took out of his lair, knowing he needed air. In his dreary, isolated days out in space the cosmos were far different. "What to do?" He says to himself, while noticing a reflection, one that reveals him to look human. He thinks back to an early memory about what he did to Ditereixtre. Letting his parents get lost in the lava than simply watching from afar as Diterexitre floated in space. Eventually he threw him a life- line.

He only had to prepare himself. He couldn't really believe the fire, in such a way too of blindsiding him. He wasn't accustomed to that type of sneakiness, intelligence, and power. Humans, for the most part were easy pickings thus far. He had more trouble playing puppet master with the lion and Cao. Of course Diterexitre was far from an exception.

He thought again now, stressed again as well at the grip he was losing with Diterexitre. He had an odd relationship with him as his mentor and the younger Diterexitre, his apprentice. Shadowed from the truth that Sorg had watched those years ago when his family became victims of mother nature.

He walks up a mountainside, spotting several flowers. He stops mid stride, captivated by them. On the distant planet he was raised on before his isolation, he was raised in a wild garden. Yes the flowers were far different though right now that was his only truly fond memory of being with a family at all.

He becomes surprised to hear Cao Nikita coming. This is good news for him, slightly thawing the iceberg of which his heart resembles. With this he had a calm over his edgy mood. Had her dilemma disappeared?

What he couldn't tell, surprising him once more, was that he couldn't pick up on what form she was in. He was one of the only ones who knew she could become a dragon as large as an elephant. For most had seen her in either your average height of five feet or the majority of her days she was only inches, entire.

Either way, "Cao?" His tone, carefully struck. "Close to the edge. Do you feel that way?" He asked her as he turned toward her, stepping closer. Her hesitation means nothing much to him, on the surface anyway. Quirky like, he said the following, "The cats loss, and I thought he had the wisdom of nine lives." Twisted smiling to her, perceptive as they come, she senses a pinch of sincerity and pain from the cat's betrayal.

She smiles back, genuinely now, which she has not done in a long time. He does ponder why, perhaps he suspects the reason tied to the lion leaving. "You've always believed in our cause?" He asks her. "I always will." Cao says. Two seconds after Sorg continues, "What I'm trying to do, it's not harming anyone. It's only to bring my people the things they do not have. We are taking over them, for their own good." Diterexitre walks over. "Death to them." He says stepping closer to Sorg and Cao Nikita. He extends his hand out to Sorg's and they firmly shake.

CHAPTER 5

A Dragon Hawk, red and pinkish, called Driona, flies overhead of the city of Badella, the largest city in the continent of Sabonia. It is a bird of dragon blood. She's a hawk, one who was born above average size, some, luckily in this day and age would say of 'abnormal' size. One who comes from large parents, far in the northern lands beyond Frondrok's tall, icy, mountains.

Driona crosses over and under this and that in the diverse city that is Badella, a city further south than Frondrok in the elven lands. Passing under a bridge she comes to her favorite river diving in its ample supply with the speed of an arrow and flying back through the surface with two fish clasped tight in her long snout. Down an alley she flies, dropping one of the two fish off to a family huddling by a fire to keep warm.

The sun takes the time that it does to rise. Shining over the dimmest of corners, bringing light where there was so little to none before its awakening. The Dragon Hawks spirit is of miraculous beauty, of the finest, purest kind. Equally, if need be she could be as vicious as she needs to, blessed with the blood of dragons.

Once, long ago, the planet was rich in dragons, full of life and spotted all over. This day, they can be found on the poles and even rarer in the far east and west ends of the world, where once they thrived more than anywhere else.

With or without the suns help she spots a couple yelling at a husky mixed breed to sit. Others disturbed by the scene glance uncomfortably at the couple, standing by a dimming fire in a pit. She flies through. She lands in front of them aside from the dog and stares at them for a long beat.

Conveying a message that she is protecting the dog, the couple judges how to respond. She notices the man slowly reaches for one of the long branches on a nearby pile. Killing them with kindness in the hopes of showing them a better way, she does what commonly cats and dogs do with their eyes fluttering, revealing the magnitude of large pupils in her eyes, as well as her majestic, ancient presence, long tail and fiery, long, feathers.

They look to Driona in awe, still with the last bits of fear in them. She shows them that she has a freshly caught fish wrapped in her tail. She drops it down for them. Opening her wings slowly full spread. She turns away from them and breathes into their fire, igniting it for them, than flying away.

The couple is petting the dog and addressing their freshly caught fish when the woman notices paw prints of Driona. "A hook?" She can't help but ask herself out loud, baffled by the glimmering way the metal hook had to it, as though it was a thing casted out of gold.

Her husband takes a close look. "Would appear to be." Leaning in closer though not feeling any heat from the hook. "Though it's steaming, it's not hot." The girl and even the dog were closer now, right over the man holding it in one of his hands. "What's that attached to it?" She asks. He blurts out, "A string." No it's a line, she follows it down and along the back- side of the fire pit, to where, several feet later, she sees it is attached to a single feather.

"A Dragon Hawk feather, she left us a means to take care of ourselves, to fish."

They pet the dog most fondly then. Others found that curious indeed. Settling on the reason, either a blessing of calm from the Dragon Hawk, or a rising above of the individuals, coincidentally in realization of the error of their ways.

Her breathtaking wings expand so close to the fullest, landing on a rare marble balcony out of all of the stone and wood comprising the city of Badella. Belonging to a king who is soon to be known as Sabian's predecessor. King Molora, fairly old, wearing some armor, jewels, and leather attire, squeals softly to Driona. His skin ivory with traces of gray, his hair a dull blackish brown, under a simple yet exotic crown.

The hawk had spied carefully from far above the clouds. "Your report about what happened to Sabian?" He asks softly, listening to her chirp in his ear. Only a few of those closest to him have the knowledge that he believes will be the push the world needs to obtain peace. After hearing about the wars escalating on the other half of the world he knows now the time is dire.

Sabian, Drusaka, and Alderon split paths after walking up to the city of Badella's main front gate. Alderon heads towards King Molora's tower, Drusaka to his chambers and Sabian, to the seasonal holiday of Anglasa's festival by the cities tranquil riverside. A relief to him, wearing normal street clothes, trying to blend in to the crowd to better forget recent days. He hears light jazzy music with a real groovy twist being played by a band outside. He laughs to himself, feeling more alive than he has in a long, long, time.

Animals as wide a variation as imaginable are along the river, accustomed to thriving beside it for generations. Tents, alongside the partially rocky borders, where the water's edge slowly fades away to the land, all the way up to the castles walls. Stands all around pop up by the second as the festival reaches its midpoint with its wild mix of fanfare.

Molora, Alderon, and Oladiz are indiscreetly talking in Molora's and Oladiz's, The King and Queen's chamber. Driona lifts off from the balcony, flying off. Molora is speaking while hand gesturing intensely to the others. Turning quickly as Sabian, led by four guards, comes through the main door. The king of Sabonia raises from his seat, turning to greet Sabian than says, "Sabian, welcome!" The Queen stands up, as she asks, in one of the most caring and confident voices he's ever heard, "How are you Sabian?"

"Thank you both. Tired still. I'm fed up, it's time to get out there!" Sabian replies, shocking them with his passion. Aiming to help, the wizard adds, "We were able to see first hand, this darkness come over one person at a time." He than crosses his hands behind his back. The Queen, most intrigued contributes this, "Like a plague, which must be stopped at any cost."

Sabian, "Yes my Queen, piece by piece, he's been taking away our very brothers and sisters, human and elven." Sabian looks to Alderon who nods in reply, as he is about to reveal a secret that the wizard detected. "This is no ordinary magic of nature. It's as if all who fall under his spell is… possessed with a warped mind."

"I saw Diterexitre, lost." Sabian says profoundly. Molora slips in, "He has been lost a long time, I thought he was put to an end." To the surprise of everyone, as if feeling responsible for Diterexitre there is a moment of silence. Sabian than says, "This world has endured such prejudice, such hatred, it is time for that to change."

The others look to each other in contemplation, pondering alternatives than Sabian speaks once more, "Please do whatever you can to get the Treaty of Union I wrote into the public here, our only hope…is equality." Sabian proceeds to step out of the circle and away from the window as a steady, uplifting breeze enters.

Oladiz now takes a concerned look to Sabian, seeing how he is moving slow than says, "Perhaps you needs none, and some rest couldn't hurt, any of us." Oladiz looks to the others. Alderon woozier than ever yet standing nods to her. "Wise words my Queen."

Alderon takes a half a step closer to Sabian's side than says, "An astounding, foreign power, one all should be fearful of, perhaps we shall see it again before us and before not too long." Alderon for a moment looks down, remembering those lost. Sabian punches the wall and says, "I attend to!" "Only monsters would kill as we have heard." Molora asks, "Is that what we are calling Diterexitre now?"

Oladiz, "Seems to fit, he and the others we heard that were beside him. His parents were like what he has become." "Well he's turned into something worse." Sabian says as he heads towards exiting the room. "Sabian?" Alderon says. Molora than asks, "What of the humans?" Alderon takes a step closer to him. Oladiz does as well, looking to the group. "Is it true, the Magic Of The Stars is within one of them." Sabian steps closer, his hand goes to Alderon's shoulder, "It is. She saved my life." Alderon adds, "She is needed with her people." They nod to each other.

Sabian stops suddenly mid stride, turning around, "Excuse me my king, my queen, Alderon, I'm not entirely feeling myself, and time must be our ally." Molora, "Of course, as long as your sure your alright?" I am. Thank you my king, my queen." Sabian nods and turns, walking out of the chamber yet stopping half way, turning to the others to say what he must, "If its one thing that must be done, it is to find the root and cut it, if it's the last thing I do."

"You, alone?" Alderon.

"Alone." Sabian states as he nods to the others than heads out. "Amazing." Molora says. Alderon finally speaks after a long beat of quiet in the chamber. "What is?" Alderon asks. Molora replies, "Sabian is, after all he's endured he is armed with nothing but himself, and by himself." Alderon, "Not if I can help it." Molora says, "He may need to be."

Oladiz, Alderon, and Molora walk outside. Witnessing the festival fade, tents folding, stands closing, as owners and the cities clean up crew tend to the break in the wondrous festival that span sun up to sun down.

Oladiz says, "As the stars have told us he is destined to be the king of kings." Oladiz looks to him sincerely and as Molora and Alderon nod to her they look up to the sky. From out of nowhere a tall, somewhat elderly, robed figure appears. Her words spoken in a deep voice, say, "Yet are you are ready to leave us?" Familiar is the voice of their arch mage, Feltak, she who taught Alderon. "Master." Alderon nods to Feltak. Molora says, "I am." Nodding to them all, and continuing, "The world is."

CHAPTER 6

A castle of gray and black stone seems nearly lost in shadow. Inside the highest tower, Diterexitre stands in front of a throne of his main chamber. He has grayish ivory skin, a few scars on his face, elven features, short ebon hair, and wears ebon, brown, and gray leather pants, long sleeve shirt, an ebon cape, and ebon boots.

Black stone comprises the high walls and square chamber. Cao, in the form of a ebon- purplish dragon, one foot tall, who has purple and black scale like skin, and a three- foot long tail wrapped around her legs. Diterexitre lowers his hands. He and Cao look out the window, overlooking mountains and a distant forest. Diterexitre says, "It's time to take him."

Howling winds echoes as an astral projection, a mix of purple, pink and black tones comes out of Diterexitre and flies out the window as a thing, most alive, as well as most possessed.

While in the land called Frondrok, a group of houses, shops, built from a mix of wood and stone, paint the background on the cold wintery day. Massive amounts of chimney smoke from those below who are doing their best to stay warm in the arctic fill the sky. Zutsiar, a charismatic, thirty something year old Sabonian with ivory skin, not too different from you or me, wears robes over a chainmail wardrobe.

He jogs to Sabian and hugs him, "Brother!" Zutsiar says, "Sabian!" Zutsiar says, hugging him again. Zutsiar than lets go and forms a worried expression... Sabian replies, "What's wrong?" Zutisar points in the forest, "Sightings in the forest. Glad you're back?"

Sabian nods to Zutsiar. "At the moment it feels as though I never left." Sabian becomes alert and walks toward the village, Zutsiar follows, suddenly Sabian stops walking. Sabian whispers to himself, "Diterexitre?" Zutsiar, "We suspect so."

Enter Frondrok Forest

A colorful sun rises over the mountaintops. Sabian wears ebon leather, chain mail, and silver plate armor on his chest, shoulders, and knees. Sabian has a somewhat nervous expression on as he and Zutsiar approach a few hundred Sabonian soldiers, both male and female, wearing chainmail and plate armor. Sabian stops walking and leans down to adjust his boot as Zutsiar walks to the others now gathering closer.

Sabian pushes up his sleeve and looks at markings on his forearm of tiny dots between interconnecting lines, than he pushes his sleeve back down. Zutsiar places his somewhat battle worn hand on Sabian's shoulder, slowly grasping it tighter. Zutsiar whispers, "I feel as though all the world is being covered in darkness."

Sabian nods to him, gets up, and he and Zutsiar walk out to the crowd. Sabian turns to Zutsiar. Sabian says, "After this we go to Nalak." Zutsiar nods, Sabian turns to address the crowd. Sabian addresses the crowd, "Diterexitre has found his way to our homes! Striking terror across the world! I want to live free of that!"

Several elves, and a Sabonian barbarian are stirring in the back of the crowd. Barbarian, "How do you know of this!" Sabian notices several in the front of the crowd looking to him encouragingly. Sabian shouts, "Open your eyes its all around!"

Many in the crowd listen intently. Sabian says, "I will ride to ask all willing to unite! Let us put aside our differences, for too long have borders kept us segregated! Unite!" The crowd cheers loudly.

Over Frondrok Forest dusk settles on the floor. A bright moon shines on, keeping earths' oceans intact with the mystical force of gravity. Rising from the shadows soldiers of Diterexitre's and Sorg's army have spawned from man, dwarf, and elf. Many of which are half solid and half gaseous, with half elven and creature like features.

While in a different part of the same expanding forest. Vistrok A Lok Vensia, male, Sabonian with ivory skin, wearing dark blue cotton pants and shirt, stands in front of Phalia, female, Sabonian elf with ivory skin, wearing a yellow dress. Both of them are in there twenties. She sits on a blanket with her eyes closed. A lot of pink fabric hangs from trees around them.

He lowers to one knee and from a pouch around his waist takes out a small box. He opens it, revealing a shiny stone. Vensia than at last asks, with all the love in his heart, 'Will you marry me?" She opens her eyes, smiles, and they hug tightly. "Yes." Phalia says. They kiss. He stands up. Vensia, smiling, "Now, may I have this dance?" He begins dancing around comically then as if their courage had dropped to the ground, they hear a roar, one that terrifies them.

Fairly close by, observing the sunset, the way it sparkles a long a running river as though orchestrating a concert of lights. A family of four, Hekah, a young boy, Salio, a young girl, and their mother and father, all Sabonian and with ivory skin, wearing furs, are cleaning clothes, they are taking in what ever comfort they can while sneaking in peeks as the sun just about sinks past the line of sight.

"Remember at Uncle Al's when we were fishing?" Says Salio, smiling as her eyes widen. "Hekah, that was two feet big!" Replies Hekah, sticking his hands in the water and gently rubbing them.

Roaring, Diterexitre's soldiers appear in a pink, purple, and ebon cloud like mist behind them. Their mother says, more nervous by the second, "Quickly, get up the river." The children are scared seeing a part of their ancestors in the blurry, distorted like faces. They stumble as they run. The father comes out of no where, grabs Hekah and Salio in his arms and runs away, faster than he's ever ran.

A trap set for the family ensnares them in a ditch in the ground. The father falls in though is able to throw Hekah and Salio safely in front of him on the dirt surface.

Whatever these things are after his children an alarm tells him they don't come from his world.

Some distance away in another area further north an honest soul, Sabian, hears ear- piercing screaming in the distance. Without hesitation he jumps in stride, running to where he hear's the cry.

Zutsiar, tracing Sabian, attempts to follow him though a cloud of smoke that within an instant surrounds him. Much of the area by the second also becomes haunted by this not only black smoke, though subtle streaks of purple and pink as well. He calls out to Sabian though his voice is shrouded. "Brother?!" Yet there is no reply oddly, as if magic prevents it.

Beside a towering waterfall a thick mist rises around Sabian, disorienting his senses. His footing staggers, stumbling to the edge of a pond. He hears screams again. He shouts in a strong, moving voice, "Who's there?! Are you all right?!" Diterexitre's astral projection forms in front of him, dispersing an ebon energy. Overwhelmed, he falls over and passes out in one motion. The energy swirls over him.

Slightly opening his eyes, Sabian bears witness to black ooze seeping all around him. He mutters, "This...can not be... this will not be." From deep down inside him, from the core, his heart goes out to those who are in need. His pray for their well being has been answered, the Magic of the Stars comes to him. With that is a vast amount of white, red, and blue, energy streaming out of his hands, spreading out into the forest. Within mere seconds every bit of Diterexitre's magic is evaporated, the astral projection included.

Night fall's on Frondrok Forest, the planet entire rotating in what seems like an effortless manner, round the sun, with the moon, as a family, as a unit. With no need for any sound, clock- work is defined, ticking away into eternity. Light, dark, trading places when they do, melding as one as though a bond is between them. One, called life.

All the while our Frondrokian family faces a very real threat, endless hatred from four soldiers surrounding the mother, Hekah, and Salio. A vast amount of white, red, and blue, energy comes flying through the forest and disintegrates the soldier. The family sighs in relief. At a whispering level the mother says, "A miracle." Salio smiles, "Papa!? Salio, Hekah, and the mother, run to the ditch. The father is holding his leg in pain, though smiles in relief when he sees his family.

Phalia and Vensia, pinned up against a tree, hug tightly, terrified at three soldiers practically on top of them. A blinding white, red, and purple, energy comes through the forest and disintegrates them as well. Phalia and Vensia exhale out in relief.

In the distance just out of ear- shot, Zutsiar along with twenty warriors are desperately fighting dozens of soldiers. More than a dozen elves are lying on the ground. As if all their prayers have been answered, as if the gods themselves blessed this world with a furious light, Sabian's magic whooshes through for these fortunate souls, saving each of them.

A spirit, a beautiful female Sabonian with ebon skin, blue eyes, ivory hair, and wearing a white dress, walks through the forest. Sabian lies on the ground partially awake. The spirit drifts toward him. Sabian sees her and smirks. In a tranquil voice the spirit, "Don't be afraid." Sabian, barely able to find the right words, never mind any words, as duels confusion, fatigue, and heartache for his people, utters, "What, who are you?"

Spirit, "I am here to remind you that love and peace does exist. Countless souls need you, find them, find peace." Sabian, slightly coming to, "Why… me?" A fog rolls over the area. The spirit floats away. Sabian, "Wait!" He swiftly walks straight ahead into the fog.

Hearing a stirring ahead he sees a bear, deer, wolf, oddly, standing still and in an area where the fog has lightened. The bear steps forward, without moving her mouth gives' Sabian a message, "You have saved our families."

Sabian in partial disbelief, nods to the bear.

Somewhat nearby, Zutsiar says to himself, "Where are you Sabian?" Sunrise gloriously arose. Sabian whispers to himself his brother's name, feeling his presence is not far, "Zutsiar." He whispers. Whatever it was that came out of him was no illusion, it was real, and it was powerful. Zutsiar smiles upon hearing Sabian's whisper.

On a bridge that leads Sabian and Zutsiar, back into town. Zutsiar asks, "What happened back there?" Sabian puts his head down. Zutsiar He nods back to Zutsiar and walks by. The bulking barbarian, wearing furs, stops and turns around to Sabian, who raises his head and looks to him.

In a walk that makes a bold statement on its own accord, the barbarian eyeballing and questioning Sabian earlier, walks up to them, as they approach a wagon equipped with a driver. Peculiar is it, the two brothers think to themselves as they exchange a glance. Much to their pleasant surprise, Alderon, pops his head out of the cabin of the wagon. "Could not sit still could you?" Alderon says to Sabian, who than looks to his brother who are wiped out though smiles to him. "Who could?" Sabian says lowly to him.

Overhearing the following from the not too far distance, "I'll follow you, and so will my tribe." Words from the large barbarian, that do not surprise the wizard, only inspire him to no end. Sabian nods honorably to the barbarian. Now for the question of questions that has been on many a mind, the one that even a group of curious spectators of the barbarian's tribe is wondering as they come over shoulder of their leader. "How did you do that?" Even upon hearing the first word, 'How', the others look around to each other as the barbarian tribe's leader looks to Sabian wide eyed.

In response, the king to be answers best he can, "I don't know." Says Sabian of Frondrok, than because the warrior struck a cord with him he adds this, "If you'll follow me, understand, you are needed most here." The barbarian nods to Sabian and walks to his tribe entire, waiting in a large clearing at the town's edge.

Alderon gets out of the wagon and heads over a few paces to his friends. Zutsiar, "Are you all right?" Sabian, "I blacked out…feeling Diterexitre's coldness. Than lashed out." Zutsiar, "It was amazing, it saved all of us." Sabian looks up to the sky for a moment. Sabian, "Brother, Zutsiar, "What is it Sabian, brother?"

Unusually speechless, he looks to his brother in admiration. His brother Sabian has a surprisingly vacant expression, lacking that special glare as common as a stone being hard. He is pondering some of the deepest parts of himself. Sabian looks to him, saying, "After this, well I don't know what she was, though she told me…" Zutsiar, "What is it?" Sabian, I don't know if I believe what she said."

Stepping closer to Sabian, Zutsiar says caringly, "Come on out with it." Zutsiar says joshing, confident his younger brother will find it in him like no other to open up, never mind how articulate he can be. They were close as close as two brothers, two friends, ever were imaginably.

Zutsiar says, "Mother and father spoke about a light that came the day you were born I never told you of it, because I didn't want you to feel different." Sabian is stunned, eyes locked on his older brother as though time, nor anything else, mattered at all.

CHAPTER 7

Within the village of Nalak's Square Sabian and Zutsiar pass by many shops and homes, scattered throughout interconnecting streets. Many villagers, beaten up, perhaps just a piece of their souls of late... look at the warriors, stopping, staring, and chattering.

A male and female villager walk toward Sabian, both dressed in rags. Female villager, "Who are you? The villager asks. Replying Sabian, "My name is Sabian." Female villager, "Sabian... Sabian?"

A group of ten Sabonian villagers walks out of the shadows, looking around with frightened expression. Male villager, "Sabian, is the forest safe?" Sabian, "For now. Though I suggest you stay together at all times. One of the villagers who walked out of the shadows makes his way in front of Sabian, an elderly male, and says, "Are you here to help us?"

Sabian, "I can tell you I will not give up on helping you." The frightened villagers separate to show Sabian a group of children, dirty, and in rags. Sabian walks in front of the children. One young girl staring at Sabian catches his eye. The look in her balances him out. Helping those who need help, fighting those off who will not agree to diplomacy, those set on a destructive course to do anything they can to selfishly get what they want.

At this point our king to be does not fully know Ditetexitre or his companions, though a point may come later in their lives when they will be better acquainted. Sabian addresses the crowd. Sabian, "If Diterexitre and the forces he stands for comes here again, think like the wind, like the elven spirit, one cannot take away that which cannot be held in ones hand!" The villagers and soldiers cheer.

A warm air comes over the area of Nalak village- square. The sun glistens. Sabian and Zutsiar are at a fruit stand eating fruit. Sabian sees Nikoli, an intelligent looking, stunningly beautiful female, as well as a Sabonian elf, with very light gray skin. She wears a tan shirt and a light green dress. She walks with a grey skinned baby, wrapped in a thick blue blanket. She is soothing the baby by rubbing her face.

Zutsiar notices Sabian is awe struck, pats his brother on the back and walks a few doors down from the fruit stand, through a shop's entrance, under a wooden sign that says, The Black Smith of Blacks Shop'. A smaller sign in front of the door says, 'B.S o' B.S and below those scrolled letter simply the word, 'Enter'

Nikoli notices Sabian. She stands still and rubs the babies belly, making her giggle.

Sabian walks toward her…she notices his walk is heavy. Sabian, "Hello." Nikoli looks to him, "Your walk seems so heavy." Sabian is slightly caught off guard pondering that her statement for a second seemed like a question to him. "Sabian, There have been a few things deep down that we should be worrying about, trying to better."

Nikoli, "I see, and I agree. Sabian is it?" Sabian nods to Nikoli. Nikoli, "I've heard of what you have done." Sabian nods sincerely to her than asks, "Is she yours?" Nikoli smiles and stares at Sabian for a long instant before responding, "My cousins. Your family?" Sabian, "My brother is with me here, yet my parents our in Frondrok." They smile to each other and to the baby.

Inside the B. S. O' B.S shop Zutsiar walks by several stacks of crates, while scanning potion vials, weapons, and bags along wooden shelves on the wall. Totec, a young boy, Sabonian with gray skin, yet with a natural look as stone that too originates on earth, dressed in raggedy cotton clothes, enters. A fat shop- keeper, a Saboninan with dark gray skin, wipes bottles with a cloth behind the counter. Totec walks around a corner and sneaks a potion vile into his pocket.

Becoming nervous, Totec, as he feels Zutsiar's eyes. Totec walks away in a hurry though trips. The potion bottle falls onto the wooden floor, cracking and spilling.

The shopkeeper angrily walks from behind the counter. In a tough manner he grabs a small club from a shelf, than walks in front of Totec.

Shopkeeper, "You? What have I told you?!" Zutsiar walks hurriedly over to Totec, and grabs him up by the arm. Zutsiar, "My son, what have 'I' told you!? Never take things that do not belong to you." Zutsiar gives the shopkeeper a stern look. Shopkeeper, "I'm sorry. I didn't realize you are his father. I was just going to scare him. Zutsiar, "Let's go."

With all the firmness he can muster, driven by care for others that run infinitely in his family, Zutsiar is still holding Totec's arm as they walk out. Outside around back of B.S O' B.S's and in broad daylight... Zutsiar stares at Totec for a moment, contemplating. Totec, "Why did you do that for me?"

With words of compassion, Zutsiar says softly, "I too was very young like you. Why did you want that potion? And do not lie to me." The boy replies, "It's for my sister. She's sick." Zutsiar holds up his pointer finger and reaches into his cloak with his other hand, taking out a potion bottle. Zutsiar, "This is enough to last the winter." Wind howls loudly, as Zutsiar hands the bottle to Totec.

Elsewhere, not too far, Hekah and Salio are playing gleefully in the snow. Salio throws a snowball and hits her brother in the shoulder. The mother and father are scanning the forest.

Father, "The road should be up ahead." The mother waves Hekah and Salio over. They come running to her side and she puts her arms around them. Mother, "When I was your age we made statues of snow that turned to ice that far north in Frondrok the cold would last throughout the Anglasa Holiday. We read stories about the stars around a warm fire."

The family smiles, than Hekah taps Salio on the shoulder and runs off giggling. Salio runs after him when she suddenly falls in ebon ooze. Salio, "Help me!" The parents and Hekah run over and struggle to pick her up. The mother and father look to each other scared.

One of the largest villages, nearly a city, home to hundreds affected by the magic of Diterextire and Sorg. Within the walls of Kulundra and Totec's home, Zutsiar and Totec enter a wooden home. Fruit is in a glass bowl on a round, wooden table set with two simple wooden chairs. Totec, "Kulundra? I'm home!"

Kulundra, a pretty female Sabonian elf, with long dark brown hair, light, nearly tan- gray skin, wearing an earth tone skirt and baggy brown sweater, walks into the main room from a dark hallway. She has a book in one hand and a cup of steaming tea in the other. She is surprised to see a stranger with Totec.

Zutsiar smiles, "Pleasure to mee…" Kulundra cuts off Zutsiar, defensive without a doubt from pains of the past, she treads ever cautiously until the emotional state of her heart can find a new comfort zone, as all deserve, and seek, "Brother, what are you doing with a stranger?" Zutsiar, "It was my fault. I stumbled into him. I owe him…" Kulundra cuts him off, "Nothing, please, 'go'." Kulundra looks to a long sword hanging on a wall behind her. Totec, "But you don't understan…"

Finding Kulundra beautiful, charming, and intriguingly captivating, everything about her was alluring. Her eyes, her toughness on Totec, a young bit of a carefree, wild type boy, like her without his parents. Standing there awkwardly for a moment. He tried to get a smile from her, or at least eye contact from her to let her know he is smiling at her, though he doesn't get it.

Kulundra cuts him off, "That's enough Totec!" Kulundra walks to the table and puts down her things. She sees Totec grab onto Zutsiar's cloak as he turns to the door. While another, follows unique aspects of his bigger than average heart, "We must respect your sister." Zutsiar takes Totec's hand away, yet holds it a moment, than exits the door. Totec lowers his head.

Kulundra sighs. Not feeling well, which last weeks or months, either way her ill will come to know a end harmoniously by Nikoli's hand shortly after she discovers her very, very, special ability.

Nalak Village Square some time later. Sabian and Nikoli are walking by a stone shop, noticing the father holding Salio, partly covered in the ebon ooze, and Hekah, standing in front of four finely dressed Sabonian, Tokon, a middle aged male with ebon skin, Hila, a female with light gray skin, and two other council members, with ivory skin, talking indistinctly.

Nikoli, "That's my aunt and uncle. My god what's happened? Nikoli points to Tokon and Hila. Sabian, "It's why I must go." Nikoli looks to Sabian with curiosity.

CHAPTER 8

The Stones Of Nature and The Temple

In Ditetexitre's newly fond cave, inside his inner keep, he falls to his knees, stunned, in a newly found pain. Stark as he is, starker yet still is the Magic of the Stars, so it would seem. Sorg walks up behind Diterexitre. "We are only beginning my friend." Diterexitre turns, barely half his wit about him, though still able to make out the sight of his mentor behind him, extending one hand out to him.

Daylight is brightening by the moment on the Temple's road. Drale, a female Sabonian elf with light ebon skin, and Shadwell, a male Sabonian elf with ivory skin…both in heavy armor standing in the rain in front of the stone temple. They are equipped with swords, bows and arrows and even bottles of potions along their belts. On their shoulders they each have a symbol of a tree and the sun.

Hearing footsteps approaching, they begin scanning the area, spotting a trail of foot- prints that lead up to the door. Shadewell and Drale open the door. Entering the temple they see Diterexitre turning from invisible to visible before their very eyes.

Between the two of them they have seen a bit o' magic over the years, though over their combined lifetimes they stand awe struck at one disappearing. Diterexitre moves his hands in a circular formation as if probing the area. The real shocker was embedded in what happened to Diterexitre's face as he disappeared, altering hideously, revealing scars and a creature like appearance for an instant.

Drale fires a flaming arrow yet Diterexitre side- steps. A second later he throws his hands down to the stone floor of the ancient temple and vanishes before their eyes... leaving a puff of black smoke to fill the room entire within seconds. Shadwell grabs a bottle that was strapped to his belt, than hurls it at where the dark one is vanishing limb by limb.

"I'll be back!" Diterexitre's voice is frost worthy chilling, echoing in the arched ceiling of the temple. Beginning to choke some while that voice bounces from this stone to that stone leaving an imprint on them. Haunting them to their last days with a frightening feeling that is terrorizing. Perhaps they think, they've seen the devil himself. Drale summons the will to speak just after a few short breaths, "He must know the Stones of Nature are here. Shadewell, "We must warn the others."

CHAPTER 9

Nalak's Return, To See A New King

Round about a mile south east of the stream in the cozy, yet fairly poor home of Totec and his older sister Kulundra's, whose jaw drops at the sight of the potion bottle Totec is holding. She runs out of the house.

Give or take a handful of streets from the village square of Nalak ... Kulundra looks in all directions, than spots Zutsiar walking along the main road and runs toward him.

Kulundra, "Zutsiar, please wait!" Zutsiar stops and turns around. Kulundra jogs up to him. Several villagers take notice than turn back around.

Kulundra, "Thank you for this, but we cannot take it." Zutsiar, "You need it Kulundra." She's closer to speechless than she had been in years... truly, since her parents untimely passing. Kulundra, "How did you know?"

Zutsiar, "He'll do 'anything' for you. Kulundra smiles, "I'll do anything for him. He's all I have. You helped him, you helped us." Zutsiar glances to the ground and back up to her. Kulundra, "He misses you. Come and see him."

The footsteps of two individuals who are getting slowly though surely better acquainted come up the path, which is the main road to Nalak village... crossing over the stream that runs easy to west, thus road, as like a holy cross, drives from the south to north, border to border.

Drusaka and Alderon are who the footsteps belong too. Many of the Villagers nod as they see Drusaka. Villager, "Darkness plagues our village. Has the king forgotten about one of us?" One of the villagers asks Drusaka.

Sabian and Nikoli walk from a small street that connects to the main road when they see Drusaka and Alderon. Sabian stops, falling into a confused state of awe. Sabian slowly takes Nikoli's hand, and they jog up to them. Murmuring comes from a crowd of watching villagers. Drusaka reaches into his cloak, pulls out a letter and hands it Sabian.

The two of them, Nikoli and Sabian, though completely naturally, let go of each other's hand. Sabian takes the letter, looks to it for an instance and than to Drusaka, who half bows to Sabian. Sabian asks, "What's this?" Drusaka, "You must read this." Sabian slips in, "It's good to see the both of you." They both nod in retrospect, seemingly to Sabian, having something more to say.

Drusaka steps closer to Sabian, looking to the villager's still watching and whispering indiscreetly about Drusaka said the 'The King of Old'. Sabian unfolds the letter and begins reading. Sabian was speechless, gathering his thoughts, lowers the letter, looks to Nikoli, Alderon, and the villagers around him. Drusaka gets down on one knee.

All villagers kneel, as well as Nikoli and Alderon. Drusaka addresses Sabian and the crowd. Drusaka shouts, "Behold our King, Sabian! Barer of the Magic of the Stars!"

Behind doors of the Nalak Council chamber, Tokon, Hila, Drusaka, and the two other council members, sit at a table. Each wears elegant robes. Hila, "I'm just scared for Nikoli. Where is this to end, a king? And now she plans on leaving with him? Tokon, "Your thoughts council?" Elder Council member, "You must not worry so Hila. To us, our children, he brings hope." Hila, "I know, I know. It's just we are like her parents. Drusaka, "He's 'more' than any of us think. Much more. And so is she."

Inside Kulundra's home several candles are lit and half eaten plates of food are on the table. On a couch in the corner of the main room sits Zutsiar, in-between Kulundra and Totec. Totec is half asleep. Stretched over Zutsiar and Kulundra's laps. Kulundra whispers, "How can we thank you?" Zutsiar, "You already have."

Zutsiar notices Kulundra's arm and neck has small markings on them.

Zutsiar, "Kulundra, how do you feel?" Kulundra, "Okay…" Kulundra looks to the floor. Zutsiar looks to the thick book on the table. Zutsiar, "You like to read?" Kulundra replies in a soft, quiet voice, "Oh yes, very much." They share a warm smile.

In the hallway, Totec, in cotton pajamas, is squatted in the hallway, intently listening to Zutsiar whistling inside the washroom. Kulundra pops her head into the doorway and smiles at Totec. Kulundra gets woozy, than regains herself.

The guest room, Kulundra taps on the door that is partially open, to the guest room.

Kulundra, "Hello there. May I come in?" Zutsiar turns, lifting the rest of his shirt over his head. "Of course. Thank you again for the room for the night. Kulundra, "Of course. You asked earlier how I was feeling." Zutsiar becomes troubled.

A brilliant sunrise outside of Kulundra's house as Sabian and Zutsiar hug in front of the front door. Zutsiar, "It'll only be a while." Sabian, "I hope our paths cross soon." A bind that lasts with no end has forged over the multitude of years. Zutsiars one to speculate, even been known as someone to be able to conjure a spell, one spell that can open like a tree does to many branches. Focusing on star gazing his life entire, to what can exist, though in his wildest imagination he has not foreseen what has already came to his planet, planet Earth.

CHAPTER 10

A Union By Way Of The Sea

At the docks here in Nalak the tides sway. Nikoli, Sabian, and Alderon, ride on earth tone Dragon Horses, a species half horse and half dragon, to a docked ship. Several other wooden ships are tied up along the dock. Alderon Drusaka is in front of a shop handing a hooded trader a small sack of coin.

Aboard a ship in the cockpit, Alderon is asleep. Drusaka sits across from him, looking at the stars. They are on a twenty- foot wooden sailboat, anchored in a large, flat, body of water. Drusaka stands up, hearing the voice of Diterexitre. With no trace of him being present, a similarly chilling effect marches up the cleric's spine, "Your new King will not save you."

Drusaka looks away from the stars and into the cabin at Sabian and Nikoli, sitting at a small table talking I discreetly. The cleric can't help but repeat the words he has just heard. Yet still he looks onward. Nikoli wears brown and tan leather armor on her chest and joints, and dark brown boots and gloves, and together, sitting close to Sabian, they smiled. If such wonders of the world can still exist, no matter how rare, let there be an ever lasting hope for us all, no matter what.

Drusaka, whispers a sole notch above his breath, "We will see." Several scrolls are sprawled out on the table. Ones already close to Sabian, and now Nikoli, as well as his brother. "Let peace win in the end." He thinks to himself while looking back to the stars.

Below in the cabin a single lantern gives off light on Sabian and Nikoli. The one his parents, Holera and Darion named Sabian, the voice inside him says the following, "I hope for everyone, friend or not, to be happier, healthier, to have the strength to do the same, to not be led astray, for me to do all I can to help this world. For those selfish I ask them to sacrifice something to help any weak, I ask to any and all of the gods and goddesses and mortals alike."

He looks about the ship, steadily forming a more hopeful appearance, than says, "I'm glad you came with us." Nikoli, "I hope my aunt and uncle are going to be ok." Sabian, "So do I." Nikoli starts reading one of the scrolls. Sabian, "I've recently titled these...The Treaty of Unions." Nikoli, "What are they about?"

Sabian, "Ways for us to live together without borders, to connect our minds, to open up our hearts. Bringing the clerics of the world together to rid disease. Making all of our cities safer and stronger." Sabian takes a deep breath, Nikoli smiles and nods. "All cultures united as one, in all seriousness... I like it." She says to him. Sabian smiles back.

Along the shoreline, an astral projection comes out of Diterexitre, standing on the shoreline, and flies out over the sea. Diterexitre holds an old ebon book in one hand. His other hand waves over the book, causing the pages to flip. His hand above the book forms a fist and the pages stop turning. Diterexitre closes his eyes and chants. A black ooze drifts from his boots and onto the shore.

Inside the ships cabin Nikoli walks over to Sabian, looking out the oval shaped, portside window. Nikoli, "What about Anglasa? It's still the holiday." Sabian hears a clunking sound from outside.

"Did you hear that?" Sabian says, "Never mind. The holiday?" Nikoli, looking out the windows than to Sabian, "The biggest, around the corner. On our way to Alphinia and Hiltovia why not gather those who stand up for the holiday's origin, of peace, and march with us."

Sabian, "Of course Anglasa! You're right." Sabian scans over the scroll. He turns to another, and than places his finger down on it and looks up to Nikoli. Sabian, "You have a rare gift Nikoli, you have both eyes open." Nikoli looks to the lantern than smiles. Sabian presses his finger down on the scroll three times. Here it is, "If you can't see the strength in uniting together, think why you were born with two eyes and two ears... it's so you can better understand, both sides".

Nikoli turns away, and stares out the port window, becoming distressed. Sabian looks up to her, taking a step closer to her. Sabian, "A march for peace. Incredible, your incredible?" Nikoli's eyes become a little watery. Sabian, "Tell me, what's wrong?" Nikoli looks out the window. Nikoli, "When you were talking I heard the word, 'both' and thought of my parents, they were killed when I was a child." "I am so very sorry."

Outside under the fading starlight among an evergrowing nighttime sky that becomes more filled with clouds than anyone on board could remember... Drusaka and Alderon are sleeping on the side bunks of the cockpit. An ebon flame like ooze ascends into the cockpit, burning the charts on a table. Alderon and Drusaka jump up in a mess of smoke and sizzling.

Nikoli, below with Sabian look to each other in shock, "I heard that!" She says as they than run out into the cockpit. "What's going on?!" Sabian takes quick looks all over. Drusaka, "something's attacking us!" A bright moon parting two massive clouds shines in the sky, as the astral projection dives under the water. Drusaka sees it dive in the water, sending him to run below.

Underwater the astral projection cuts into the bottom of the boat with its long finger- nails. Nikoli, Sabian, Alderon, and Drusaka hear scratching from under the boat. Alderon and Drusaka run into the cabin.

Drusaka yells from below, "There's a leak!" Nikoli, "Fill it in with something!" Nikoli looks to the sail wrapped around the boom. Sabian looks where she is looking, than runs on the deck, pulls out a short sword, slices the lines that wraps around the sail and throws it to her. Nikoli catches the sail. She throws it to Drusaka in the cabin, than Alderon runs down. "Here!" She shouts.

Underwater the astral projection sprays the ooze that attaches to the bottom of the boat. Drusaka and Alderon bunch the sail in a hole of the bottom of the boat. A little water leaks in from the perimeter of the hole. They look at each other relieved, than the ebon ooze floods into the hole, disintegrating the sail. They both look at each other frantically.

The astral projection flies out of the water and toward the ship. Nikoli takes her bow off her shoulder and pulls an arrow from the quiver that is leaning up against the table in the cockpit. Sabian jumps down from the deck down into the cockpit. Nikoli, "It's coming towards us!" Nikoli aims her bow and arrow.

Alderon looks to Drusaka, "Go, help them!" Drusaka hesitates, looking to Alderon surprised. Alderon puts his hands on the ooze. A glowing red light comes out of them. Drusaka nods and runs up three steps to the cockpit. Under a full moon atop of the ships deck Drusaka runs next to Nikoli. The astral projection is flying toward them. Drusaka, "The boat is sinking!" Sabian looks to Drusaka frantically as Nikoli finalizes her aim. Drusaka glances to her, getting a strange feeling as she releases the arrow and quickly readies a second.

Drusaka whispers, "Zalingoth, Arigoth." Drusaka puts his hand up as the arrow nears the astral projection. The arrow flares in light as small symbols of golden triangles and circles appear around it. The arrow and the symbols pierce into the astral projection with a burning light.

The astral projection yells, "Aagh!" Sabian and Nikoli are shocked, looking at the symbols still floating in the air for a few beats than fading. The projection hovers, groaning as the burning light disappears. They see the ooze now over the bow, disintegrating it.

Sabian, "It' spell eating the boat!" Sabian quickly climbs onto the mast and lunges onto the astral projection, causing them to splash into the water. Under water Sabian wrestles with the astral projection as the ooze begins to surround him. Nikoli is running from place to place looking over board.

"Sabian!?" She calls. Drusaka runs onto the deck where the ebon ooze is spreading. Drusaka, "Nikoli get Alderon above deck!" Nikoli runs to the stairs that lead below, she turns around, shouting, "Sabians alone!" Ina sharp reply Drusaka replies, "Don't worry! Nikoli hurry!" Nikoli runs down the stairs. Drusaka steps to avoid the ebon ooze though it approaches fast, burning his boots. Drusaka, "Agh!"

Following Nikoli, Alderon and her jog into the cockpit. She sees that the ooze has eaten away at the entire bow area, creating a massive amount of water over to pull the boat under.

Drusaka is on his knees, straining to keep a blue light shining from his hands, holding off a bit of the ooze. Nikoli looks to the small wooden lifeboat that is tied onto the stern of the boat. Nikoli, "Into the lifeboat!" Underwater the astral projection pulls Sabian toward the propeller of the ship. A second before they hit into the steel propeller Sabian pulls the astral projection into it. The astral projection screams out while dissolving away.

Inside a lifeboat Drusaka, Nikoli, and Alderon pull Sabian out of the water. Once in the safety of the shabby, yet sturdy, wooden lifeboat Sabian catches his breath. His shoulder has claw marks on it. Sabian, looks to Nikoli, "Are you all right?" She nods yes, than looks to Drusaka's boots sizzling and Alderon, a bit exhausted. Nikoli, "What was that thing?" Drusaka, "I could feel it was a part of one named Diterexitre." Sabian grows highly confused, and utters, "Part of him?" Drusaka, says, "In a way, a projection of him."

Nikoli is distressed, "That thing looked like what killed my parents. What does it want?" Drusaka looks to Sabian, "Our new king." Several beats of silence pass them as they look at Sabian. Sabian to Drusaka, "What were those symbols?" Drusaka, "Clerical symbols." Nikoli is stunned, "I... don't know... You're saying I'm a, healer." Drusaka nods to her. "Sabian reaches for an oar though grunts, than holds his wound. Nikoli puts her hand on his shoulder.

Slightly relieved, Sabian looks amazed at Nikoli and nodding thanks to her. She nods back, looking to Drusaka next. Sabian asks, "What of Diterexitre, I heard he had been defeated long ago?"

Drusaka grimaces than nods, "We discovered Diterexitre's lineage sought after a very rare way, Dark Magic. When he was young he and his parents traveled north and encountered an erupting volcano. That day the Dark Lords parents died, and the boy who was a elf began his own path."

Flashing back in time to Ditetexitre's castle. Drusaka continues, "An army of soldiers stand in front of his castle, made in part with a mountains base." Diterexitre, appearing in his twenties to thirties, walks out of the main gates. He walks in front of the army of soldiers, in rows on either side of the gates.

"An army of thousands of Elves, Sabonians and Alphinians, stand across. The Hiltovians were nowere to be found. They charge each other." Drusaka's voice is heard as he tells the tale. "He survived the volcano, and raised an army of darkness beyond anything his parents ever imagined. Many died. We had enough tears, enough victims. Hundreds of sorcerers silently surround the castle, each wearing cloaks or robes. Inbetween them a thin beam of yellowish blue energy forms, connecting them."

Drusaka continues, "Our Council agreed where steel had failed only magic would prevail. We surrounded his castle with every magic user we could find. We began casting the Spell of Ages. The beam of energy focuses into one gigantic ray that shines onto Diterexitre's castle, making it explode, pieces floated into space. We learned that he was on one of the pieces. He flew through the darkness of space, yet his powers lashed out, killing the sorcerers."

Back on the lifeboat, in the present time, Drusaka, Sabian, Nikoli, and Alderon, are on the lifeboat, spotting the shore. Nikoli and Sabian look to each other somewhat shook up. Alderon puts his hand on Sabian's. Alderon, "What he wants with you is what you stand for, our hopes."

While in a not to far off area, the astral projection slowly re- enters Diterexitre's body. He stands on the beach shore, groggily. Diterexitre, surprised, says, "My lord?" Sorg, as an undistinguished figure, surrounded in a black glowing light descends towards him, looking up and seeing now his faint elven facial features. Sorg hovers slightly above the small waves crashing on the beach, "Why are you here?" Ditetexitre asks.

Sorg holds out his hand and out comes three dark glowing balls. The balls lower to the shore, two of them form into bodies, Drexzulath and Lituluka. They have elven and beastly features, and many with a shadowy mist around them.

Sorg says lowly, "To help you." "What of the human woman?" Diterexitre asks. "She will come to us." Diterextire nods to Sorg as the third ball now changes into a body, Vilanowa's, who looks similar to the others do, yet something him is very different as though caught more between his elven and human side. Diterexitre stands stronger, looking to each of them. Sorg disappears as a black gas spreads wide in the sky.

CHAPTER 11

Nalak's Return, A Welcomed Messenger

Zutsiar, Kulundra, and Hila, are looking at the strange ebon in the sky. Zutsiar notices that the markings on Kulundra are larger. Zutsiar, "Do you feel any different?" Kulundra looks down, Zutsiar follows her eyes, looks at Kulundra's markings, "I've noticed many getting sick." Zutsiar contemplates.

Standing by in the door- way, Zutsiar notices the family Sabian saved walking by with baskets of vegetables. Salio looks weary…She is being carried by her father. Hekah, "What about dessert?" The mother replies, "Your sister's favorite, strawberry shortcake. The mother and father notice Zutsiar and smile to him. Zutsiar smiles back. The family walks down a street. Zutsiar looks to the clouds overhead.

Driona, the fiery red, pinkish Dragon Hawk, breaks through the clouds, screeching prehistorically. Zutsiar, "Fly. Tell Sabian Nalak is in need of a healer, great need." Driona takes off fast. Many villagers around the area look at the Dragon Hawk and Zutsiar, somewhat hopeful.

CHAPTER 12

Of Elves Of The Sea

In Port City, bordering Sabonia and Alphinia, Sabian, Alderon, Drusaka, and Nikoli walk from the life- boat, tied up at a dock. Around the dock they go until in front of the largest tavern in sight. A gathering of Sabonian diplomats talk indistinctly, passing by the stone sign above the tavern says, 'Dragon Horse Inn', which is mounted above double wooden doors.

Hundreds of elves were out and about in Port City, even some Hiltovians and varying dwarves. Drusaka, Sabian, Alderon, and Nikoli, walk up a small nearby platform beside the tavern. Nikoli and Drusaka are holding up scrolls. Several hundred if not more are of the locals of the city gather round the podium, excited, nervous, curious, about the rumor of a new king.

Proudly Drusaka raises the scroll high over his head, "He with the Magic of the stars is to be our king!" Nikoli steps forth, adding, "Join us across the world to support the Treaty of Unions! To form peace in spirit of Anglasa!" Sabian walks to the very front of the platform. The villagers gather closer and many cheer.

Ban, a Mountain Dwarf, four foot nine inches and stocky, takes his helmet off and excitingly looks to Sabian. Ban, wearing stone armor, makes his way through the crowd toward Sabian. Sabian, "Isolation separates us from our neighbors, our brothers and sisters! Only together will we be strong enough to end Diterexitre's terror! Imagine, Sabonians, Alphinians, Hiltovians, Dwarves and Dwelvens, with one voice, an equal one!"

Ban, "We'll follow you King Sabian!" The villagers cheer wildly. Sabian sees Ban, with one arm waving at him and the other pushing through the crowd. Ban, "Sabian!" Sabian sees him, "Ban!?" A sigh of relief hits Sabian.

Simultaneously Alderon, Nikoli, and Drusaka say, "Who?" Sabian turns around to them, "An old friend!" Nikoli, Alderon, and Drusaka smile. Inside the Dragon Horse Inn dozens of elves chatter among the funky music of an Alphinian band playing. Drusaka Alderon, and Ban are on line at the bar.

At a table with five chairs, Nikoli and Sabian sit, whispering indiscreetly. Sabian, "Since the moment I saw you…" Sabian attunes to the vibe of the tavern as three Alphinian messengers, one purple skin, green skin, and blue skin, though all very pale like beige skin mixed with those earth tones, and wearing heavy armor, enter through the main door.

They walk to the bartender. Nikoli sees Sabian looking at the Alphinians. Nikoli whispers, "Time has its way with us." He smiles to her. The three Alphinians talk discreetly with the bar tender. Drusaka, Alderon, and Ban walk to Sabian and Nikoli. Drusaka, "My King?" Sabian reluctantly looks away from Nikoli and up to Drusaka.

In the heart of Port City, Sabian, Nikoli, Drusaka, Alderon, Ban, and the three Alphinian messengers, are standing at the end of the dock, looking at an elegant riverboat pulling up. Sabian takes a tightly rolled scroll out from a sack over his shoulder. Dozens of Alphinians Elves armored, pull in the long oars, preparing lines to dock.

Quinatal, a lean Alphinian with blue skin, long ebon and blue hair, wears elegant armor, and appears to be sixty years old, sits in the center of the boat. Drusaka, "The Alphinian King." Drusaka looks to Sabian and the others. Sabian stares at a flag with a blue sail above a colorful seashell, blowing in a strong wind atop of the mast. Four light purple, yet earthy, skin Alphinian's help the messengers tie up to the dock. Quinatal stands up and walks onto the dock. Quinatal, "Grustinul Isok King Sabian."

Sabian speaks in the Alphinian language, "Han Isok King Quinatal." Quinatal, and all the other Alphinians are greatly surprised. The sun twinkles as Sabian gives a greatly curious expression to Alderon, Nikoli, and Ban. Quinatal, Drusaka, and others notice the sun brightening. Sabian walks to the edge of the dock. One of the Alphinian messengers steps closer. Sabian holds his hand out and meets Quintal's with his. Drusaka walks beside Sabian.

Quinatal "You speak old Alphinian?" Sabian "I believe I do." Quinatal curiously looks to Sabian and Drusaka, than nods to them. The king of all the seas and oceans in the known common world, spanning thousands of miles, and representing his wife, Queen of Alphinia, he speaks his traditional language, "Irv han erhul, om kulopin von dal Alphinian ond vilhwo drankan."

"The sun shines even brighter. On behalf of the Alphinian people we welcome you." Sabian hears the words, is able to translate them to his language of the common new tongue, his gut speaks to his mind, trusting in himself, his instincts, and miraculously connecting the stars and vast knowledge they hold, all via his magic. Sabian replies, "Wu kommel bal quatre bal jonnen Diterexitre."

Quinatal, proper and trusting, as the legends about him tell… Quinatal says as he takes a single step closer to the Sabonians, "We will join you, against Diterexitre and all odds." Sabian bows to Quinatal. Drusaka, "King Quinatal, may I ask how you heard we were here?" Quinatal, "Word travels fast in our ocean, and we too know the time is right."

In the cabin of the most elegant ship, with natural decor of the ocean around them, Sabian, Drusaka, Alderon, Nikoli, and Ban, are sitting around a table. The cabin is finely decorated with statues, candles, glass lanterns beside porthole windows, and paintings of underwater scenery.

Nikoli, "How can you speak Alphinian?" Sabian, "I'm not sure." Sabian shrugs his shoulders. Alderon states, "Our Arch Mage Feltak pitched to our council that the Magic of the Stars, is remarkable, it must be. The 'need' has pushed it forth to this day, where language can no longer divide us." Ban, "What have you become my friend?"

Sabian looks to Ban surprised, like a deer caught for an instant in the headlights.

Quinatal walks into the cabin. Quinatal, "Our flagship awaits us." Sabian turns to Quinatal and start to stand up. Drusaka replies, "We are honored King Quinatal."

On deck of the humungous ship justifiably named the Alphinian Flagship, the group sits in the cockpit under broad daylight. Sabian, Quinatal, Ban, Drusaka, Nikoli glance around as hundreds of Alphinians are in arms, walking and tending to the ship; coiling rope, swabbing the deck, and cleaning assorted spears in weapons racks along the walkways. The ship is enormous, anchored among a few smaller ships. Quinatal, "Your treaty reads fair. What has given you these ideas?" Sabian, "They are part of me. Nearly my every thought."

Quinatal stands up, as Sabian turns around and stares off the stern of the ship. Quinatal looks over the ships stern while saying, "I believe there is strength in you…enough to follow." Sabian turns back around and nods

to Quinatal. Sabian, "Please, the most honorable of Sabonian greeting"...
Sabian reaches for Quinatal's forearm, Quinatal does the same, and they
shake forearm to forearm. Quinatal, "It is my honor." Sabian turns to the
stern again.

Sabian nods to him, than says, "We fight against time, Diterexitre grows
every day."

Quinatal points ahead, many of the crew look to him and says, "Set
sail to the kingdom!" The crew jumps to picking up the anchor and within
seconds four sails unwrap from the three masts, and a massive propeller off
the stern spins fast.

Sabian and Quinatal stand on the bow. Crew tends to the ship, full sail
and moving fast. Dozens are readying catapults on the sides of the ship by
the weapons racks. Quinatal, "For the first time in my life, of more than a
thousand years. I feel I have found one worthy of following to the depths of
Diterexitre's domain.

Quinatal looks at Sabian for a few beats. Quinatal looks out to the
darkening water, distressed. Sabian, "What's on your mind?" Quinatal, "We
have heard of a dungeon?" He looks away from the water and to Sabian.

The Liege Alphinian King, appearing nearly human and elven somehow,
says awfully concerned, "The rumor say millions are there, and call it a
place of horror. A place that Diterexitre keeps cloaked, hidden from all."
Sabian unravels his sleeve and shows Quinatal markings on his forearm. The
markings are tiny dots between interconnecting lines, which begins to glow
bright. "I have these markings for a while now, somehow I know now why."

Quinatal leans over to study Sabian's arm. Sabian, "Call it crazy, but a
spirit spoke to me about countless souls needing to be saved." Quinatal looks
to Sabian with extreme curiosity. Sabian, "Than there's this, like voice, inside
me that says this will take me there." Quinatal nods to Sabian, looks to the
stars, than looks back to Sabian, now looking to the waves hitting. "Believe
in yourself, I believe in you, and if anyone can find these people, it's you."

Within the hallway of the vessel, hundreds of feet, Sabian walks, passing
several doors, than stops and softly taps on one of them. Sabian whispers as
to not wake anyone up, and honestly not wanting to bump into anyone who
refers to him at all, never mind my lord, King, High King, or anything accept
his name, "Spphh, Ban it's me." Inside the room Ban was sleeping until the
tapping, he groggily turns around in his cot, squinting to see the doorknob
turning.

Ban springs up to open the door.

Sabian, "Ban, I'm sorry to wake you." Ban sits up, waving Sabian over. Ban says, "Is everything all right?" Sabian walks to the bed and sits down beside him. Sabian sighs, taking a deep breath. Ban, "Hey it's me, what is it?" Sabian relaxes and smirks to Ban. Sabian pushes himself to convey his torn self on the surface, admitting, knowing his inner side. Where his core strength derives is making the right decision about what he is going to say, "I must go. There is something I must do, alone. When I've gone I need you to keep things together until I return. Nikoli, though she's quite the fighter, needs nobody... I..."

Ban interjects, seeing his old friend struggling, comforting however pops to mind, Ban states, "I will watch over her with my life for you my friend, you have my word, though remember I can come with you, than to rally the dwarves. Alderon could watch over your, 'loved ones'

Awkwardly Sabian blushes, trying to express his next words carefully as his heart races, he kicks himself and spits out some words, trying to find sense in it all, "Love? I don't know if I love her, ok, ok, I might, I think I do, at least what I know of her so far I..."

At that moment, Sabian hesitates ever so briefly. Ban takes the liberty in being the friend Sabian has chosen. After all since they were teenagers, practically living next door to each other. The dwarf reaches down, taking great pride more so now after seeing how Sabian further feels about it and says, "I'll do it Sabian, after all we were practically neighbors growing up."

Sincerely nodding to Ban, Sabian turns to walk toward the door. He stops when just an arms length from the door and says, "As for rallying your people, I'm all for it if they are open to it, once I've returned. Once I've gone, tell the others to meet me in Badella, and thank you my friend." Later that night Sabian is standing in front of a closed door. He is about to knock, though doesn't, than slides a note under the door.

CHAPTER 13

The Next Stage, Of A World War

A breathtaking sunlight to warm even the coldest of hearts awakens over the blue ocean. A Sabonian war ship with hundreds of Sabonians, ivory, gray, and ebon skin, both male and female, makes headway, even with smaller sails than the Alphinian Flagship. All onboard wear an assortment of silver armor and leather and tend to guard duty or sailing the vessel. A female, ebon skin captain walks behind the elf steering the helm in the cockpit. A male commander, with ivory skin, stands next to the helmsman. Captain, "Commander, full speed ahead!" Commander, "Aye Captain!" Dozens of the crew are scurrying in tightening the sails.

While aboard the Alphinian Flagship one of the crew pulls on a line, hoisting their flag up along the main mast. Quinatal gives the one who raised the flag a hand signal. The elf nods back and unwraps a sack at the bottom of the mast and pulls on a line that it is tied to. The sack unravels the Sabonian flag that has a triangle in the center and three smaller circles aligned around it. The two flags are side by side at the top of the mast. Nikoli and Sabian stare at the flags blowing in the wind. The other Sabonians onboard are happily surprised. Sabian smiles to Nikoli, and says "Our flag."

Nikoli smiles to Sabian and he to her. Sabian walks toward Quinatal. Sabian, "United, it's a good feeling." Tolomal, a female with light green skin, long ebon and blue hair, wearing coral plate armor, walks out of the cabin and beside Quinatal. Quinatal sits in a large seat behind the steering wheel. Tolomal, "There is another vessel on our course."

Quinatal walks beside Sabian. A scout in the watchtower on the mast shoots a smoking arrow in the sky, than it dissolves. The scout hand signals to Quinatal in the direction he fired. Quinatal pulls a scope from his belt, and sees a Sabonian warship, scout, "Sabonians!" Quinatal hands Sabian his scope, Sabian looks through it.

From the Sabonian ship atop a watchtower on the mast, three archers fire flaming arrows at land, where a few hundred soldiers are aligning on the coast. Aboard the Alphinian ship all aboard on deck see the flaming arrows and the soldiers on the coast. Dozens ready spears and halberds. Nikoli readies her bow and arrow.

The flaming hot arrows streak through the sky, striking nears the soldiers. Lituluka, in shinny, charcoal plated armor, holds his arms up in the air as all of the soldiers swarm into the water and fly into the air toward the ships. Lituluka "All strike!" Quinatal, "Sabian, let us sail to your warship!" Sabian nods to Quinatal. Dozens of Alphinians tend to the sails as the helms-elf slightly alters course. Sabian runs up to the bow of the ship, getting a better view of the soldiers.

Sabian, "There must be five hundred!" Dozens of hideous, half dead as well as alive soldiers appear in swirling, whirlwind, puffs of pink, purple, and ebon smoke above the ship. The soldiers spray rays of fire and ebon ooze from their hands while swooping down and stretching out with their long talons. The Alphinians throw blades and fire rocks and steel balls at the soldiers. Quinatal, "To the skies! Defend High King!"

Most of the Alphinian crew is surprised at Quinatal's command, though throw spears at the soldiers nearing Sabian. The Alphinian ship drops anchor and it's sails as it pulls up beside the Sabonian warship, also dropping anchor and it's sails. The Sabonian captain, "Protect King, board the Alphinian warship!" Hundreds of Sabonian knights, both male and female, run and jump onto the Alphinian ship and head toward Sabian. Alderon, Drusaka, Nikoli, Quintal, Ban, and Tolomal, are attacking the soldiers coming from all directions.

Drexzulath, wearing similar armor to Lituluka, appears by Lituluka's side in the center of the horde. Drexzulath and Lituluka are in front of the remains of the horde. A few hundred more soldiers appear behind Lituluka and Drexzulath in a pink, purple, smoky cloud that fades away. Drexzulath, "Cease the High King!" Alderon, Nikoli, Ban, and Drusaka run behind Sabian.

Sabian, "Stay together!" Sabian points to the nearing horde, more than a hundred catapults and sharply tipped arrows from the Sabonians cut into them. Soldiers on the ships tear down dozens of Sabonian and Alphinian elves. Quinatal is swinging his battle-ax wildly at soldiers around him. Lots swarming all over the deck though block several Alphinians run toward him.

In secrecy, the Prince to Alphinian, in blue, green, highlighted in a shiny purple, full plated armor, wearing a face- plate, battles a circle of soldiers with a halberd. He tries to get closer to Quinatal. Sabian runs toward Quinatal. Quinatal is knocked into the water by a group of soldiers. Sabian is about to jump in the water after Quinatal when Drexzulath, Lituluka, and two large soldiers appear in front of him. Tolomal and Alderon run to the side of the boat and look into the water, than become surrounded by several soldiers.

Nikoli shoots two arrows, each burn into the soldiers they strike into as those hear a faint chiming sound nearest. Tolomal, "Lord Quinatal is overboard!" Several Alphinians acknowledge Tolomal and dive into the water. Tolomal swings a halberd and kills a soldier. Sabian swings his sword wildly at the soldiers. Drexzulath backs them away, snarling in fear at the High King's animalistic style. Ban notices Lituluka running behind Sabian.

Two soldiers appear in front of Ban. Ban, "Sabian look out!" Sabian looks behind him though Lituluka grabs hold of him with ferocious, deceptive speed. Tolomal, "Archers defend King Sabian!" Drexzulath readies a spear to throw at Sabian. Sabian looks to Nikoli, surrounded by many Sabonian knights, and Ban, fighting several soldiers. Sabian wrestles out of Litulaka's grip just as Drexzulath hurls the spear. Sabian ducks to avoid the spear as a Sabonian knight dives in front of it and is stabbed in the chest, "My king!" The knight shouts as she falls to the ground.

Sabian, "No!" Sabian grabs the knight with the spear in her chest as her eyes close. Lituluka takes down a handful of elves running over. Sabian looks at the elves fall. Drexzulath raises his hands, an ebon lighting comes out striking Sabian. Sabian recoils from the pain, still lying the knight down. He than lifts his head high, turning in a rage to Drexzulath. Drexzulath fires another bolt at Sabian, yet he puts his hands in front of him, grunting while stepping toward him. Deflecting the bolt back at Diterexitre's lackey, causing him to not only stop firing though crash to his knees. Drexzulath cowers, "Agh!"

The fierce warrior in Nikoli calls out, "Sabian!" Spotting his struggle though again another soldier appears before her, viciously raising its long jagged sword over its head. Alderon struggles with soldiers. Lituluka comes from nowhere and tackles Sabian into the water. The blue, purple, and green armored Alphinian cuts down the last soldier in front of him than dives in the water.

Underwater dozens of soldiers swarm over Sabian as he grabs Lituluka's throat, causing him to loosen his grip. Drexzulath swims toward Sabian. Alderon, Ban, Drusaka, and Nikoli surrounded by soldiers appearing in puffs of dark hued smoke. As well underwater, Quinatal, alone, has eyes a glow in an ebon fiery light. He bleeds heavily. In the distance he sees Sabian surrounded. Alderon, Nikoli, Ban, and Drusaka, still aboard and cutting down the last of the soldiers around them.

Ban, "Come on!" Alderon, Nikoli, and Drusaka dive in the water, along with a few dozen Sabonian knights. Many knights and soldiers on the ships are bloody, wounded, lying down cringing, though some are fighting still. The Sabonian captain slashes the last soldier near her, "Commander hold the ship! A squadron with me!" Says the captain.

The captain dives in the water. Nearly fifty knights, some wounded, follow him, some ripping off their helmets and chest plates before diving.

Possessed by a foreign power, Quinatal swims toward Sabian in a mad rush. Lituluka, Drexzulath, and several soldiers, each of them appearing more human and elf up close than Sabian noticed earlier. They grab onto him. Alderon grabs Drexzulath from behind, burning him and causing him to drop his spear. Sabian slashes three soldiers down with his sword. Lituluka grabs Sabian and they wrestle over his blade. Nikoli stabs one of the soldiers, than another, with a glowing arrow.

Drexzulath shakes Alderon off than waves his hands in a circle, causing ebon electricity that makes Alderon flinch. Drusaka wrestles with Drexzulath as a dim blue light spawns from his hands. Behind Lituluka's shoulder, Sabian sees seven Alphinian knights swim to Quinatal. Sabian is traumatized that Quinatal is bleeding heavily. Quinatal raises his battle- axe to bring it down in a series of deadly slashes that befall knights around him, both Alphinian as well as Sabonian. Sabian becomes distracted, giving Lituluka an opening to push the blade within an inch of him.

Five Sabonian knights swim to Quinatal, who swings in a wrath at them, taking all of them to their demise. Sabian becomes raged, a white, red, and blue energy swirls around him...burning dozens of soldiers around them and making Lituluka and Drexzulath wince. Quinatal swings at Drusaka and Alderon, who just barely ducks out of the way of his battle- ax.

Nikoli, an Alphinian knight, and a Sabonian knight, tackle Quinatal. Quinatal rips the Alphinian off of him though drops his battle-ax. Quinatal punches out the Sabonian knight, than grabs the Alphinian knight with one hand and Nikoli with the other and chokes them.

Dozens of soldiers besiege Drusaka, Alderon, Ban, and the other knights. The red, white, and blue energy still disperses off of Sabian's body as he swims to Quinatal and tries pulling each of Quinatal's hands off of Nikoli and the knight. Sabian lets go of Quinatal's hand holding the knight and uses both of his hands to free Nikoli. Quinatal grabs Sabian's throat with both hands, clenching, squeezing with the fury fueling the darkness overwhelming his once pure nature.

Split seconds before Sabian passes out his energy glows brighter, striking Quinatal, causing him to let go, and to disintegrate him. Drexzulath and Lituluka disappear, while the other soldiers are burned to a crisp by blinding magic of the High King, Sabian. Above the surface, atop the warships over a hundred wounded Alphinians and Sabonians are trying to fend off the soldiers.

To the rescue with mere moments to spare Sabian's white, red, and blue energy breaks through the water, smoldering all of the evil soldiers. Releasing them one by one from their tortured captivity of being under someone else's control. The elves show great surprise, followed by sighs and smiles full of relief. Sabian is treading water while the knights swarm towards him. Spurts of energy disperse from his hands, trickling along the water as he himself is a star sizzling.

Sometime later the crew tends to repairs; hammering, sawing, carrying crates. The wounded are lying on the deck on cots. The blue, purple, and green armored Alphinian, has his helmet under his arm, sitting beside the still body of Quinatal. Dozens of Alphinians mournfully watch over Quinatal. Sabian walks beside Tolomol, staring at Quinatal from up on the bow. Drusaka, Nikoli, Alderon and Ban sit near Quinatal, tending to their wounds and such.

Sabian, "Who is that beside lord Quinatal?" Tolomal, "His son, Prince Mar." Sabian looks down to the ground. Tolomal, "The Dark Lord's spell on Quinatal was merciless. You did what no other could, you saved us." Sabian looks up slightly. Sabian, "If only it didn't come at such a high price."

Tolomal, "Please, come." Several Alphinian knights form an opening in the crowd around Quinatal and Prince Mar as they see Sabian and Tolomal headed their way. Mar wears the blue, green, and purple armor, and has light blue skin and long greenish black hair in a pony- tail. Tolomal, "My Prince,

King Sabian of Sabonia, and the High King of Elves." Mar turns from Quinatal and walks slowly to Sabian.

Sabian leans in close to Mar. "I'm sorry for your loss." Proceeding to speak as gently as he can, "I'm sorry it was I." Mar takes a deep breath, looking round to the destruction around them, "You saved us. My father, lost control, Diterexitre will pay."

Tolomal looks to many others who have settled their attention on Mar and Sabian. Tolomal, "Praise our champions, King Mar of Alphinia, and High King of Elves, Sabian!" Tolomal raises one of Mar's and Sabian's hands into the air. Everyone onboard gives a roaring applause. Sabian looks to Mar, who gives him a friendly nod, Sabian nods to him than addresses the crowd, now all watching. "First we are to kneel, for those we lost!" Sabian bows his head low and kneels. All others mimic him.

That evening in one of the guest quarters of the Alphinian ship. Nikoli picks up the note left for her, sits down on the bed, unfolds it, and begins reading; 'Nikoli, I'm sorry to not have seen your face one more time before having to go. I have gone to free those imprisoned. For only you understand 'our' treaty, as I do, Hiltovia awaits us." Nikoli puts the letter down on the bed, sighs, than smiles. She says to her, "I'll do my best."

CHAPTER 14

Titans Clashing over Freedom

Diterexitre walks through an arched doorway into a hall. Lituluka and Drexzulath follow him. Diterexitre walks near the window to where Vilanowa stands, staring outside. Diterexitre turns to Drexzulath and Lituluka, looking them up and down. Drexzulath, "We took many, even King Quinatal." Replying sharply, Diterexitre, "The High King?" Drexzulath reluctantly shakes his head reluctantly and responds in a low voice, "He fought as though possessed."

Vilanowa, remains composed, which Diterexitre thinks is suspicious. Drexzulath speaks up, "We will fight harder my lord." "Yes you will. The three of you." Vilanowa's looks up catching wind of Ditetexitre's explicit message to him as well as the others. The time is relative of course, though he and Vilanowa exchange a brief stare down than Vilanowa nods to him. Diterexitre, Lituluka, Drexzulath, and Vilanowa are on dark skinned, Dragon Horses, riding out of the gates implemented in front of the cave. They look to an army of thousands of soldiers. Diterexitre, "The next phase. We begin anew hunt."

CHAPTER 15

The Guardians of the Stones

A wooden ship, about thirty feet long, barrels through the water with one large front sail. Drale and Shadewell are steering the wheel under a heavy rain. They look to the thickening clouds above them. Drale, "What do you make of this?" Shadewell, "The end is near!" Drale, "Get a grip Shadewell! We're almost there!" Drale points towards mountains in the distance. Her charisma fair, slight over weight, tall frame, surpassing Shadwell by an inch, yet her backbone stronger than his.

Just at that moment a black gas forms from the clouds and lands over them. Black ooze than starts eating at the deck. Drale looks down to Shadewell's steel boots, gripped into the wooden deck by their tiny spikes. Shadewell, "It's Dark Magic! Drale, "Those boots will be all that's left of us if we don't jump!" The boat dissolves quickly. Leaving a black gas in its place, as the black ooze seeps into the water. Shadewell and Drale jump in the water.

Not too far away on land Drusaka, Alderon, Ban, Nikoli, Mar, and Tolomal, are the head riders of several thousand warriors and villagers. Hundreds hold up signs that say, "Treaty of Unions", "King of Stars", and "Our Savior". A party of villagers begin singing, "Anglasa is here, joy to everyone, everywhere! Anglasa is here, another year, Anglasa shine bright... every night in starlight." Nikoli turns to them and smiles to the villagers singing.

Afternoon in Badella city, decorated with ornamental lights, layered by a huge sign above the main gate that says "Happy Anglasa." Four knights in full plate silver armor and face- plate helmets, open up a gate in the center of the wall. Zutsiar, Kulundra, Tokon, Hila walk out of the gate and onto the lawn to where Tokon and a few thousand Nalakian villagers stand. Driona is atop of Totec's shoulder. Many villagers are coughing. Tokon addresses the villagers.

Driona flies atop of Zutsiar's shoulder and squawalks in his ear. Tokon, "Chased from our homes! I say we can stay here in Badella, under the protection of the King's army, and live another day to see our homes again!" The Nalakians cheer.

Along the main road to Badella, Drusaka, Alderon, Nikoli, Mar, Tolomal, and Ban, ride on horses along a curvy, large cobblestone road. Ahead of them is a fork in the road to Badella or due east. Several thousand Alphinians and Sabonians are walking behind them, some of which are riding on horses. Drusaka, "The fork, to the right Badella, to the left Hiltovia...where we part ways, my Queen." Nikoli, "Queen? Sabian and I are not..."

Nikoli stops. "I'm sorry my lady I didn't mean..." Drusaka humbly apologizes for striking a nerve. Replying Nikoli says kindly, firmly too, "No, it's ok. He didn't even say good bye." Drusaka, "He loves you Nikoli, that is all I know." Nikoli smiles to Drusaka. Nikoli, "I hope we meet again Drusaka." Drusaka smiles to Nikoli.

Ban rides beside Nikoli. Ban, "A friend, asked me to go with you, lady Nikoli."

Nikoli shakes her head no, giving him a stern look. Drusaka, "Even if you insist Nikoli, he'll follow. Nikoli smirks to Drusaka and Ban and races off. Ban hurriedly follows.

Upon the shores of Badella's coast within a forest's trail in broad daylight Drale and Shadewell limp. The ebon ooze is around them on the ground and their clothes are soaking wet. Drale looks around, "The spell is here too?" The ooze creeps around one of Shadewell's boots. Drale pulls Shadewell's arm though the ooze spreads up his leg. Shadewell, "Go to the road for help." Shadewell greatly strains, Drale runs down the path.

Where the forest ceases meeting the edge of the road to Badella, a flower bunch here and there stretches for life in between the ooze. Zutsiar rides his horse hard along the curvy road with the city of Badella behind him. From the other direction Nikoli and Ban ride their steeds along the curving road approaching the fork. They are surprised when seeing the ebon ooze dripping from the treetops in front of them.

They look around to either side of the road. They hear footsteps getting louder. They slow down. Ban grabs his long handled battle-ax from behind him. Nikoli readies her bow and arrow. Drale, partially covered with the oil colored ooze, comes running out of the forest just in front of them. Nikoli, "My god." Diterexitre. Drale, "Diterexitre." Drale, woozy, falls to her knees. Nikoli and Ban scurry off their steeds, running to her. Nikoli notices a symbol of a sun on Drale's shoulder.

Nikoli, "She's a Guardian Knight!" Drale points into the forest. Nikoli nods to Ban, he runs into the forest. Nikoli holds Drale up. Nikoli, "It's alright." Nikoli touches the ooze on Drale, making it most of it fade away. Nikoli sighs though is fatigue struck a bit. Drale feels better. Ban comes out of the forest holding Shadewell, who is barely breathing and covered with the ooze.

Riding hard along the road when he sees Nikoli and Ban, Zutsiar, "Ban?!"

Zutsiar rides towards Ban, Nikoli, and Drale, just than they see Drusaka, Mar, and Tolomol come riding up to them. Badella's outer city wall is where Zutsiar and Feltak stand in front of the open city gate.

Kulundra, Tokon, and Hila, stand behind Nikoli and Drusaka who are in front of a line of hundreds of Nalakian villagers. Standing on the head of the line holding up Shadewell and Drale is Alderon, Mar, Tolomal. Drale struggles to lift her head up. Drale, "The Dark Lord remembers the Stones of Nature." Feltak, "They are as one, Sorg, leading Diterexitre further astray." Drusaka, "He's been lost since childhood."

Nikoli, "No one is truly lost."

Drusaka realizes the severity of Nikoli's words. Drusaka looks to Nikoli and nods to her. A meeting of the High Council of Badella is held in their chamber...Feltak, Alderon, Drusaka, Mar, Drale, Shadewell, and Nikoli are in the chambers sitting down. Nikoli and Drusaka are exhausted, and sipping water from glasses and talking indiscreetly.

Nikoli, "Enough, I must head to Hiltovia, the longer we wait the more Diterexitre gains. If all your talking about here is about what Sabian, what the High King wants." Drusaka, "Nikoli is right." Nikoli stands up, though stumbles a bit. "Have you the strength?" Drusaka says. Feltak, standing up, "The road ahead from Sabonia to Hiltovia, to long, given our urgency. There is another way."

In the castle of Badella, the words 'Chamber of Travel' in letters half the size, below that, 'created by the Dwelvens', is etched onto a wall of the chamber. A large triangle is engraved on the stone floor. Standing in the triangle are two hooded Sabonians with their arms held out wide.

Feltak and Drusaka lead Nikoli and Ban into the center of the triangle and than look to each other. Feltak raises one of her hands. Feltak steps closer to Nikoli, "You'll reappear in Hiltovia. Ban steps closer to Nikoli than says, "With limbs intact?" Drusaka lowly laughs. Feltak, looking down to Ban, "Indeed, and perhaps longer."

Ban, Feltak, Drusaka, and Nikoli smirk, as well as a few of the hooded elves. Nikoli says proudly, "Thank you Feltak." Feltak, "Ready yourselves." Feltak signals to the hooded elves, they raise their hands together, forming a faint, rainbow between them. The light covers Nikoli and Ban and they disappear as Feltak steps back.

CHAPTER 16

The Darkest Dungeon

Dusk paints shades of blue marvelously mixed with black tones as Sabian rides his steed up a jagged cliff. At the top of the cliff he pauses, gazing at stars in the clear sky flaring. His eyes, just for two seconds, glow with a blue, red, and white light. He climbs down from the steed. He whispers into the steed's ear. They walk in different directions.

In the mountains canyon he walks among icy winds, layers of heavy snow- fall on his defined shoulders. He looks up to the sky, no longer seeing the stars. To his surprise he notices his markings glowing. His hands as well as face have blisters from the icy temperatures. He walks further, toward a shady, narrow path between to massive mountains.

Night arose over the mountain- tops, home to many Dwelvens, those who have elven and dwarven characteristics; pointy ears, bluish gray skin, white beards, fairly short, wearing thick furs, and rock and silver armor. Asate and Barok, Dwelven sorcerers, are in earth toned, moderately colorful robes. Asate holds a scope to her eye, with Sabian in her sight.

Collapsing to his knees Sabian falls. The snow is three feet high in every direction. He closes his eyes. The battering winds pound hard on him. A few beats pass, he opens his eyes and stares to the mountain- tops. He scans them suspiciously.

He gets up slowly and limps. Relieved, he sees a small cave up ahead. In the constructs of a man made cave centuries ago Sabian is huddled on the ground. He moans, looking at his frosted hands. He achingly wiggles them. He pulls out a small loaf of bread and unwraps it.

Sunrise sparkles over the mountains as Sabian climbs along a mountain cliff. Looking up into the sky he sees the sun bright. He reaches a plateau, catches his breath and looks through his scope. He sees a faint image of Diterexitre's castle. Foggy gas around the castle camouflages it into the clouds that have fashioned.

Up to Diterexitre's cave like castle Sabian walks. Night- falls over his backside as he spots large grates in the ground by the main gate. He strolls to the gates just then giant pink and black astral hands encircle him. The hands grab onto his legs, pulling him to the ground. Sabian yells out, "What the... Agghh!"

Sabian struggles to get free, pulling his sword out. More astral hands arise over his hand holding the sword. High up in the mountains under a partially full of stars type sky in the a few dozen dwelvens run down the cliffs toward Diterexitre's dungeon.

Barok walks beside Asate. They raise one of their hands into the air. The dwelvens halt, taking aim with bows and arrows and cross bows. Sabian is in excruciating pain as he is pulled in different directions by over a dozen astral hands. The grates begin to crack.

Barok lowers his hand. The other Dwelvens release dozens of arrows, while they are mid air Asate says, "Wer Sund Fuer ind Ferba." The arrows suddenly flare in green, blue, and yellow as they fly through the air.

Sabian's hands burst with the red, blue, and white energy, disintegrating a few of the hands. The arrows strike into what's left of the hands, causing them to retract back under the grates and scream out in ghostly like echoes of twisted souls. Sabian looks all around in shock as the light around his hands fade and the arrows evaporate. Sabian, "Who's there?" Yet he sees no traces of his in part saviors.

Sabian limps to the backside of the gloomy castle where he notices a small tunnel.

Long, spiraling, forged as an escape route, he walks hunched over down a tunnel under ground. Endless seems the path, covered in mud and rubble, crawling through an ever-tightening hole. A pile of rocks, accompanied by dirt, collide on top of him.

CHAPTER 17

The Queen of Queens

In the unique environment of a desert merged with a wild jungle in Hiltovia, Nikoli and Ban walk into a clearing. They see a city made in part with rolling sandy hills. Nikoli, "Hiltovia." Ban, over looking the view, says, "Land of the most arrogant people in the world."

Directly outside the King Of Hiltovia's castle, Nikoli and Ban stand in front of the enormous sand- stone structure, with a feeling as if they have been there for ages. Lifeless, large shadows reflect their mood as they await a greeting. The ground is covered with red, orange, yellow, sandy rolling hills. Ban, "I've never felt less invited."

The gate opens vertically, from top to bottom, and out walk two large Hiltovian knights. They have yellow skin and heavy armor, holding long staff axes. One of the knights, in a raspy voice, says finally, "The King cannot see you in." Nikoli and Ban look to each other, Nikoli, "Did you tell him we come on behalf of Sabonia?" Hiltovian knight, "Yes."

The knights turn away and walk back. "And the Queen?" The knights pause, look to each other than continue walking away under the gate, shutting behind them with a thud.

Nikoli and Ban look at each other in shock. Coming up to Nikoli and Ban is a Hiltovian scout, dressed in average street clothes with only leather shoulder pads, "Lady Nikoli?"

Startled, Ban and Nikoli look around yet see no one. The scout with light orange skin whispers, "I speak for Hiltovians who would hear you. Please follow me." "Who are you? If this is a trick…" The scout jumps in, "It's not,

Kilique of the rebel alliance, requests you." At this point the warm tones of the sun shine brighter than they have in a long, long time, cascading over the floor of the ground as they distance themselves from the denial of admittance moments ago. What matters is that they, Nikoli and Ban are there for a reason bigger than whatever it was, or is, bothering themselves. Nothing really could have prepared them for what set their nerves on edge from Valinor's dismissal.

High up, towering above all adjacent vantage points stand a circle of a hundred Hiltovians, in sand stone- armor, and dozens in earth tone robes on steeds. Standing beside them on a maroon dragon horse is Zet, a female Hiltovian, with light red skin, wavy brown hair, and a fine silk shirt under steel armor, in her thirties. Kilique, Hiltoivian with pale yellow skin, wearing mostly leather and cotton cloth, is beside her.

CHAPTER 18

The King's Struggle

Inside one of the tunnels in Diterexitre's castle Sabian's hand appears out of a massive pile of rubble. He crawls further, hearing voices murmuring. Turning a corner, his unbreakable spirit pulls his body to crawl further... into another passage that opens up to a large rocky clearing. A crumbling noise from behind alerts him, he turns around as a giant stone falls on him as literally a gigantic part of the ceiling collapses. Pink and green giant astral hands are on the top of the stone pressing it downward.

CHAPTER 19

Badella, King and Queen

Two knights, wearing full plate armor and face- plated helmets, stand beside the door of the chamber to the High Council. Feltak, Alderon, and Drusaka stand in front of the large bookshelves. Feltak is holding a large old book. Alderon, "Nikoli showed me the note the king left, he'll need help. Please Feltak, one more time." Feltak, "What we did earlier, we did in the hope that the Hiltovians will join the Kings alliance, signing his treaty. Besides, now we are far too worn." Alderon, "I'll go by steed!"

Alderon throws his arms up and walks toward the door. Drusaka, "Wait Alderon! We ready for war. Scouts tell us he has been slaughtering villages." Alderon stops walking and lowers his head, "What does he want with Sabian?"

Feltak says, "For him to be out of his way. We believe with enough magic Diterexitre can bring back those he lost. He could strike here. He remembers the Stones of Nature. Who knows what else."

Feltak throws the book down on the floor. Alderon lifts his head and turns around.

Feltak, "His magic has clouded us from seeing his plans, or where his castle is." Alderon rebuttals, "Forgive me, but this is madness..." Alderon turns, looking now to Drusaka, "You've taken great steps to tell Sabian of his destiny, and now... The king is alone." Drusaka, "Perhaps he needs to be." Alderon walks out of the room.

Along the Badella road Alderon rides fast on a black horse. Up in the sky he sees a trail of some sort. He takes it as a sign, perhaps even a map to his friend. He smiles to himself, riding the horse harder. Along that very same road the Nalakians camp has hundreds of tents and campfires. Zutsiar has a sword strapped behind him. He indiscreetly talks to Kulundra when to his surprise he sees Alderon cruising by.

Back in doors inside the thick stone- walls of the High Council chamber Drusaka and Feltak are at a window looking at the hard rain pouring on the city, full with decorations, lights, and a melodramatic music played on the streets below. Feltak, "What of Alderon, he was Sabian's friend long ago, but can we trust him to bring him back?" Drusaka, "I can trust him, for it was he who brought him back when Molora and Oladiz wished it. I feel a strong will within him." "What of the kind and queen of old?" Drusaka asks. "They have gone, leaving no trace." Feltak says softly, looking up into the heavens.

Feltak turns from the window and looks at the book on the floor, and slowly bends down to pick it up. Drusaka, "We could lose the city to a blinding attack. Diterexitre has been to the temple, we have our warning."

Feltak closes her eyes just as Drusaka turns to her. Drusaka speculates, "He could have found a way to take the stones. We must send the army." Drusaka steps up to Feltak as she reopens her eyes. Feltak, "No. We will not send an army. The Capitol city would be at risk of falling." Drusaka shouts, "Better the city than the world!" Feltak, "Sorg and Diterexitre would detect that as a weakness to our defenses, my word is final."

CHAPTER 20

The Queens Treaty

Broad daylight joined by a misty cool breeze, crisp as spring pushing to let winter release it's freezing like grip over the land, tries to shine over the Hiltovian mountains. Nikoli trails behind Ban. Ban has his battle-ax in his hands. He has long blond, wavy, hair that blends into his beard. Approaching the top of the mountain Ban sees the Hiltovians. Ban, "Nikoli, he speaks the truth, it's a gathering!"

Ban waves for Nikoli to come ahead. Atop the plateau of the mountain, Zet, and Kilique ride their horses a few paces up. Chatter of those in the circle silences when seeing the scout, Ban, and Nikoli now. Knights near the scout step outward, allowing them to pass.

Kilique, "Greetings Nikoli, Ban, I am Kilique of the Hiltovian rebels. This is Lord Zet, and the Guardian Wizards. Nikoli and Ban look at each other astonished.

Kilique, "Forgive the mysteriousness and welcome to Hiltovia."

Nikoli nods to Kilique, bravely walking up to him, taking a scroll out of a leather- over shoulder bag and holding it above her head in one of her hands. Ban looks around at the others, each as still as the next, than follows right behind her. Nikoli, "I speak on behalf of King Sabian of Sabonia, High King of Elves, who seeks a union with Hiltovia.

Nikoli lowers her hand. Many of the knights chatter. Zet clears her throat the knights get quiet. Zet, in a deep warrior born voice states, "I have heard of Lord Quinatal. King Sabian was responsible for his death." Kilique interjects seeing how Ban and Nikoli become uneasy, "Lord Zet, please." Zet takes a step forward, as Nikoli and Ban tense up. Zet, "I remain skeptical, after all King Molora has left in a time of war."

Wafiroth reveals a wooden staff from his robes and slams it to the ground. Wafiroth, "Enough, yet we are here for one reason, to stand with the elf of the prophecies. He with the blood that comes from the stars, and that is not Valinor or Quinatal."

Most others in the circle nod. Nikoli walks up to Zet, looking at the others around her, attentive. Nikoli, "I quote the High King's treaty, "If you can't see the strength in uniting, think why you were born with two eyes and two ears, so you can better understand 'both' sides."

Nikoli turns from Zet, than stops to lift her head up high, turning in Zet's direction. Nikoli, "You heard wrong. Sabian saved everyone when Quinatal was turned against his 'own' soldiers. Sabian was the only one who could have stopped him, who could have saved him." Kilique than Wafiroth, Spair, Rainerie, otherwise known as Rockeri for his connection, his deep- rooted power of the Earth, and Zet, climb down from their steeds and walk to Nikoli. Zet, "I understand."

All the others look to Nikoli surprised, and nod to her. Zet, more respectably, "Where is King Sabian?" Nikoli, "Diterexitre's castle." All are stunned. Talk rises among the circle. Wafiroth puts his hand on Nikoli's shoulder, nodding to her. Nikoli forms a satisfied expression. The sun flashes dark and bright again. All look around the sky with confused expressions.

CHAPTER 21

The Light in Darkness

Trapped in Diterexitre's castle, Sabian strains to lift the giant rock…the astral hands, beyond Sabian's sight, press down stubbornly. One of the beaten up, dirty, innocent prisoners utters, "Who's there? Help us." Another despairingly says, "Move, that wall is cursed!" Sabian hears the voices, encouraging him to strain greater…sending a white, red, and blue energy seeps out of his hands, and a very thin trail of it out of his eyes, wrapping around the stone. The astral hands are surrounded by the energy as it cinders them. Sabian hears footsteps as the energy around him disappears.

Behind the bedrock thousands of prisoners are crammed in a very dark, dirty stone area. Dozens are by one of the stone- walls, partially covered in dirt. Most of the prisoners are lying down on the ground or looking to that wall. The first prisoner who spoke says, "Someone else is coming."

In the tunnel Sabian sees Alderon and Zutsiar jogging toward him. They help Sabian try to lift the stone. Zutsiar, "Can we help?" Sabian, in a straining voice replies in utter shock, "Brother, Alderon, how is this so?"

The three of them strain to lift the giant stone yet it raises only a little. Alderon, exerting himself, "We followed a trail in the sky with Driona's help, we thought it could only be yours." Zutsiar notices Sabian's arm has markings on it that are glowing. Zutsiar, "Your arm?" Sabian remarks, "It led me here." They hear a cry for help leaking through the very old stone itself, a prisoners voice, and a child's voice, "Help us please!"

The astral hands reappear behind Alderon and Zutsiar, grabbing hold of them. A much brighter red, yellow, and blue light emanates from him. The astral hands burn away and cry out as Sabian pushes the stone up all the way. Dozens of flocking soldiers flying down the tunnel at their backside become disintegrated by the energy. Above the castle of Diterexitre the sun flashes very dim and bright.

CHAPTER 22

Hiltovian Lords

Day shines on in one of its last hours over the Hiltovian castle. Behind the wall are tens of thousands of Hiltovian villagers and warriors gasping as they are surrounded by darkness, than a bright light from the sun. Not quite as high as the clouds, on the castles rooftop looming over Hiltovia is a large sandstone tower. Overlooking the city King Valinor, a Hiltovian with yellow skin, a thin gold and red crown over his medium length brown hair, stands with five Hiltovian lords with red, yellow, or orange skin.

Valinor wears dull bronze armor, and each of the commanders wears robes, mixed sandstone armor, and like Valinor they appear to be in their early sixties.

The lords are worried, looking out the window. A Hiltovian lords says, "King Valinor, its Star magic. Valinor walks briskly to the window, looks up and sees the sun with a swirling white energy around it. "The Sabonians." He says lowly, with an angry undertone.

CHAPTER 23

Tides Turning

Out of the window of the High Council chamber Drusaka and Feltak stare. Seeing the sun has a swirling white energy around it. Below in the city streets there are thousands of villagers staring up into the sky. Drusaka, "Sabian." They smile to each other.

Far north, hundreds of dwarves decorate the mountain, each, of female and male Mountain Dwarves, three to five feet tall, have fair length hair, gray, ebon, red, and brown, wear stone armor, and stand on mountaintops looking to the sun with a swirling white energy around it.

Sabian takes flight, breaking through the ceiling of the dungeon with a loud crash. Pieces of the ceiling fall down into the tunnel, though the white, red, and blue energy lights around the debris, cindering while the tunnel illuminates.

Alderon and Zutsiar, lying on their backs, in shock at the large hole in the ceiling. The energy dissolving the stone- wall in the tunnel without delay... Sabian hovers above Diterexitre's castle, looks to the necklace glowing, and flies up higher. He throws the stone down onto the main gate of the castle. The gate crumbles. He notices the sun has a swirling white energy around it, as his hands glow brighter.

In Port Cities main square Diterexitre notices the light around changes looks to the sun, seeing a swirling white energy around it, and a thin trail of red, blue, and white energy in the sky. Diterexitre stands among thousands of dead elves and a smoking city behind. He angrily strains, than glides away from the city.

Lituluka and thousands of the dark alliances soldiers look to Drexzulath, pointing at Diterexitre gliding away. A basement to a family, one hard working, one clinging to all that remains of themselves, keeping them sane, wishing the madness of the reality swirling around them would go away. They hide together, several children huddling together with a few teenagers.

An adult, Sabonian, couple, male and female, and two mid aged women, look out the single small basement window at the terror outside. An elderly lady sitting on a crate is next to the children, struggles to get up. One of the teenage boys helps the lady up. The elderly woman says in a low frightened voice, "To the window dear boy."

The elderly lady grabs hold of the teenager's arm, and he helps her walk to the window. He asks, "Grandma, what do they want?" The woman replies, "Evil has little meaning darling."

Miles upon miles away, inside Diterexitre's castle, lingering of the haunted, countless deaths, Zutsiar and Alderon see prisoners standing or lying on the ground through the opening of where the wall was. Alderon steps through the opening. Alderon, "Your King has freed you!" Chatter among the prisoners is louder and louder as they look in awe at Alderon. Zutsiar, "So many?"

Hundreds of thousands of prisoners walk out of the castle, wounded, limping, and carrying each other. Alderon walks to a corner of the castle and stops. He sees horse prints heading off into the mountains. Alderon, "Our steeds?" Sabian lands in-between Alderon and Zutsiar. Sabian, "Is everyone all right?"

Alderon replies, "Most, hundreds of thousands were here. Are you?" Sabian, "Yes, I wish we came earlier, to save them all." Zutsiar, "How is it you can fly?" Sabian, "I think it's the very stars themselves." Zutsiar adds, "You did well brother." Turning to the masses of prisoners walking out of the main gate. A few of which strike down a handful of Diterexitre's soldiers frantically yelling indiscreetly.

Noticing the crying in the background, the High King walks toward them than notices pieces of burnt, silver, plate armor lying on the ground partially covered in dirt. Sabian walks up to those crying being consoled by two others. Sabian, "What is it? You are free."

One of the prisoners utters, "Most of us have been here for years." Sabian looks at them sadly as the female prisoner cries and says, "Our daughter. So young." Sabian looks to them with curiosity. Sabian, "Daughter?" A hopeful expression forms on Sabian. The male prisoner says, "She was all we loved." Sabian, "Please, tell me her name."

"Nik. short for Nikoli." They say together. Sabian grins than says, "Nikoli, of Nalak!" The two crying prisoners, in their late fifties say in sync. Sabian, "She is alive!" The two prisoners flutter Sabian with a tight hug, saying, "Really?" Nikoli's mother asks.

Sabian senses something and looks up in the sky. Nikoli's mother says, "Do you know where she is?" Sabian, "You have to go, now." They look at each other confused.

Sabian flies fast to the head of the line of prisoners, where Alderon and Zutsiar are leading all away from the dungeon. Sabian shouts out in a panic, "Diterexitre is coming! Bring them to Badella. I'll give you the time you'll need." Alderon, "Are you crazy? Alone!?" Zutsiar asks, "Brother are you sure?" Sabian, "Go please! Protect them!" Sabian wearily races off, grabbing the chest plate armor from the ground.

Sabian says to himself, "Nikoli, I've barely told her how I...love her."

CHAPTER 24

The Queen in Closing

Far away, on the Hiltovian road, Nikoli rides on a brown horse when seeing the sun get brighter. Sabian's voice is heard inside her mind, "...How I love her." Nikoli replies, "I love you too." Ban rides with Wafiroth, Spair, and Rainerie just behind Nikoli. Further back, Kilique, ride in front of several thousand footprints, and a dirt cloud.

CHAPTER 25

The High King's Stand

Back at Diterexitre's dungeon Sabian stands, weary, wearing the armor. He sees Diterexitre eagerly walking in his direction. Inside Sabian's mind he hears Nikoli's voice, "I love you too." Sabian looks up into the sky and smiles. Diterexitre is about fifty feet away. He and Sabian stare at each other for a few beats.

Sabian faces Diterextre, "You're destroying our world!" Diterexitre calms his face. Sabian looks around while taking a few steps closer. Opening both arms wide, Sabian says, "Let us talk, please." A glare comes to Diterexitre's eyes, pondering Sabian. Diterexitre, "'Talk?', I haven't heard that word from an elf in a long time."

"It can be again. I am the King now." Sabian says. Diterexitre, "Much has changed. I am not the same elf I was." Sabian walks closer, surprised at Diterexitre's words. Sabian, "Please, put all that behind." Diterexitre walks closer to Sabian. Diterexitre, "Why are you here?" Diterexitre looks around, noticing the main gate crushed and gets angry.

Sabian, "All I want to do is talk." Diterexitre, "What have you done!? They were taken to be freed." Sabian, "They were taken against their will. They have the right to choose when and where they go. You say it's been a long time since another, wanted to talk? You do this?"

Diterexitre, "I was banned from my homeland. Called a murderer!" Diterexitre casts an ebon energy from both of his hands at Sabian. Sabian tries to dodge it by flying up. Diterexitre casts it wider as it hits Sabian's chest plate. Sabian cringes out in agony, "Agh!" He falls from the sky, crashing to the solid ground. Grunting, Sabian opens his eyes wide, shooting a white, red, and blue energy from his hands, striking out at Diterexitre, causing him to shout out, "Aghhh!"

Diterexitre moves his hands around, disappearing into thin air. Sabian looks around. Diterexitre reappears right in front of Sabian, reaches out and grabs his throat with his twisted soul. He tightens both hands around his throat tighter. Sabian reaches for his short sword strapped to his leather belt. Diterexitre squeezes tighter, making Sabian close his eyes and strain to the point of passing out.

A loud thunder and flash of lighting gets their attention. Diterexitre loosens his grip.

At the mountain -side, standing together are the Dwelven sorcerers. The sorcerer holds a Dwelven baby wrapped in a blanket. The sorceress holds a wand over her head, which triggers dozens of lighting bolts from the sky. Asate, "Together we give you hope Sabian, as we know you will give us a bright future."

At the dark lords castle a lighting bolt strikes Diterexitre, creating crackling sounds. He cries out and releases Sabian's throat. Sabian falls to the ground, holding his throat and gasping for air. Diterexitre falls weak on his knees, entering his mind is a memory as a young boy, with his parents, Lopah his mother, and Loran, his father, surrounded by lava erupting from a volcano.

His father has ivory skin, long black hair, and wears a leather shirt, pants, and boots, similar to his mother with dark gray skin, and wearing a black dress. Lighting and thunder occur. Diterexitre looks up in the sky and sees an image of Sorg, snapping him back to the present time... in pain, a different time, an on all fours, while Sabian crawls away toward a nearby cliff.

Somberly, Diterexitre says, "Why were you there?" Sabian, confused, hears Diterexitre curiously, turning his head around to look at him. Observing Diterexitre is stunned, he hesitates, yet sees thus as a chance to regroup. He crawls down the cliff, while seeing Diterexitre hold his head with both hands. Sabian turns from Diterexitre and makes for the cliffs drop-off.

He rolls down the cliff, becoming battered by the rocks. He falls and catches his roll a few times before reaching the bottom. He than lies still for several beats, opening his eyes slowly and starts to get up. Rising up Sabian, limps along a dirt road ahead.

Bruises and small cuts all along his legs and arms. Asate's voice is heard as a long range of echoing weaving its way in endless waves of sound. Each spiraling molecules in the air between her lips and his ears near, "If you ever need us you know where we are."

Sabian's ears pierce up, points and all, looking around though sees no one. He stops limping. Sabian, "Who's there?" Regaining himself a little, Asate appears a hundred feet in front of him. The sorcerers hold one of their hands out to Sabian.

Asate, "We speak for the race of Dwelvens. We know you will give us all a future." Sabian is stunned at the sight of the Dwelvens, takes a beat and than smirks to them, nodding thanks.

By the outer wall to Badella two Hiltovian soldiers blowing horns, riding steeds under Badella's main gate opening. Nikoli, Ban, Wafiroth, Rainerie, Spair, Kilique, follow them, with a few thousand Hiltovians at the tail.

Five hundred armored Sabonian knights and five hundred Alphinian knights stand guard on the outside of the main gate, each attentively staring at the Hiltovians.

Within the quiet walls of Badella's High Council chamber Feltak looks out the window over looking the new comers approaching.

Drusaka, Oladiz, Tokon, Hila, Mar, and Tolomal stand behind her. Feltak, smiling says, "The Hiltovian Rebels, and Nikoli." Tokon and Hila hold each other's hand and smile. Near the tall walls of Badella's inner wall the Hiltovian army stands behind Kilique. A few moments later Feltak, Mar, Shadewell, and Drale greet Nikoli and the others by the inner gate.

"Welcome to Badella Lord Kilique, Nikoli." Says Feltak nodding to her. Kilique, "We have come to fight for the King of the Stars." Shadewell and Drale have bandages on them, walking to greet Wafiroth, Spair, and Rainerie. Spairo, "It is good to see you. Why have you come?" Wafiroth asks, "Diterexitrre." Replies Drale. The single word sends chills down to all who hear his name. In realization, Wafiroth, "Come, we must race to the temple."

An ebon skinned Sabonian scout, wearing ebon leather, rides up to Feltak on an ebon horse. Scout, "High Mage Feltak, we've spotted Alderon and the King's brother approaching with a large following. Feltak, "And the King?" The scout shakes his head no. At dusk on the outer side of the gates to Badella, Alderon and Zutsiar trot up to the road to the outer gate, leading tens of thousands now free elves; Sabonian, Hiltovian, Alphinian, and hundreds of dwarven.

Drusaka commands, "Bring food and water!" Dozens of Sabonian knights run off. Alderon and Zutsiar ride up to Drusaka and Feltak. Drusaka most concerned inquires, "Where is King Sabian?" Zutsiar, "I hope he follows." Nikoli's eyes are waterier as she lowers her head.

Behind the inner wall of the city hundreds of Sabonian, Hiltovian, and Alphinian villagers and knights hand out food, water, and blankets to the thousands of elves and dwarves. Feltak and Drusaka are standing in front of the crowd on a platform. Nikoli wipes off some tears, than hears chatter and crying from the crowd. She sees some of the knights walking in that direction and follows them.

She hears her fathers voice nearby, "Nikoli? Does anyone know a woman named Nikoli?" Nikoli hears her than frantically starts to make head way through the crowd. Nikoli, "Mama? Papa?" Ban, Zutsiar, Kulundra, and Totec notice Nikoli.

Crying and smiling at the same time Nikoli pushes further through the crowd. Nikoli's parents notice her. Nikoli's mother excitingly asks, "Nikoli! Is that you?" Many of the crowd turns as they notice Nikoli. Nikoli, "Papa!" Nikoli and her parents embrace in a long hug. Nikoli, crying, "Mama, I thought…" Together her mother and father say, "I know, I know." Zutsiar, Kulundra, Totec, and Ban, smile as they watch Nikoli hugging her parents.

At the outer gate three Sabonians, one with ivory skin, one with gray skin, and one with ebon skin, three Alphinians, one with blue skin, one with green skin, and one with purple skinned, three Hiltovians, one with red skin, one with yellow skin, and one with orange skin, each holds a flaming torch and wears earth tone robes, standing in a single line in front of the outer gate.

"We await the King, with all our prayers." Feltak, Oladiz, Mar, Tolomol, Drusaka, Ban, Kilique, Nikoli, Tokon, Hila, Kulundra, and Totec, wait at the end of the line in front of the center of the gate. Night falls over Badella as Sabian limps toward the outer gate. Millions, between the prisoners and all the warriors he has united thus far stand holding torches. The guards stationed at the outer gates kneel to Sabian, and one of them blows a horn. All see Sabian and are shocked as to how beaten up he is.

"Commander!" Drusaka shouts pointing out to Sabian. The Sabonian Commander standing nearby on his horse, beside a Dragon Horse, races off. The commander jumps down and helps the King up onto the Dragon Horse. They trot up to those holding torches and all kneel. "Those you have united my King." Bowing to Sabian the commander respectively gets down from his horse and kneels.

Sabian, half out of it, puts his hand on the commander's shoulder, climbing down from the steed. In the corner of his eye he sees Nikoli and her parents standing by Drusaka.

Nikoli and Sabian run to each other. They kiss and hug tightly. Sabian takes Nikoli's hand and lowers to one knee. Sabian looks up into her brilliant blue eyes, as the prettiest thing he has ever seen, than with all the love in heart, asks, "Will you marry me?" Nikoli, for an instant speechless, smiles and replies, "Yes."

Sabian stands up and he and Nikoli kiss again. They turn and smile to her parents, both happily crying. Sabian holds up Nikoli's hand with his and looks out to the crowd cheering. Drusaka and Feltak walk up to Sabian. Feltak reveals a steel crown and holds it up above Sabian's head with both of his hands. Feltak places the crown on Sabian's head. Feltak, "Our King! Our Queen!" Wildly the crowd cheers once more "Hurrah!" All stand up continuing to cheer. Popping out under the moon- light henceforth are more stars appearing in the midnight sky

CHAPTER 26

War's Brink

In a mountain canyon Zutsiar, Kulundra, Alderon, Drusaka, Feltak, Ban, Mar, Tolomol, Zet, and Kilique trot in the front lines of a army; comprised of thousands of Sabonians, Alphinians, and Hiltovian knights, barbarians, and robed elves trotting on earth-tone horses. Sabian and Nikoli are standing a few hundred feet in front of them all.

Sabian, "You have accomplished a miracle in Hiltovia. Kilique and Zet seem as noble as any. They tell me that King Valinor marches against Diterexitre. We'll await him here, making a union with him one way or another."

Nikoli, "Valinor or their Queen would not even see me." Sabian reaches out and holds Nikoli's hand, contemplating. He waves Drusaka forward. Drusaka trots his horse beside Sabian, "Yet because of you, he knows we will not give up. I must talk to King Valinor before he arrives, it cannot wait. I'll meet you back here."

Flying off of his steed and into the clouds, Sabian disappears. Ban, Zutsiar, and Alderon, ride up to Nikoli and Drusaka. Zutsiar, "What did you say to him?" Drusaka, "I, uh…" Nikoli and the others look up to the sky.

Behind the walls of Diterexitre's main chamber he himself is sitting in a throne, thinking. Soldiers, in steel armor, stand still along the perimeter. Drexzulath and Lituluka enter. Diterexitre, "What have you learned?" Drexzulath, "The Stones are lightly guarded." Diterexitre, "The fools! I should have taken them! Go now, and bring them to me."

Nearby, among the clouds Sabian is flying fast, over mountain- tops, even small villages. Asate's voice enters Sabian's head, "Sabian please hear me?" Sabian hesitates, than stops flying and hovers. Sabian, "The Dwelven?" Asate replies, "Asate is my name. A vision of Diterexitre revealed him seizing the Stones of Nature. Their guardians will not be enough. If he gains them all would be lost."

While in Hiltovia, on the rooftop of his castle Valinor stands with a handful of lords looking at a map. Valinor, "I have sent General Kroko to Diterexitre's land." Hiltovian lord, "How will they find the hidden fortress?" Valinor, "That is a secret." The lord's form impressed expressions as they look to each other as well as glancing to Valinor. "We will join them tonight." Valinor says confidently.

Sabian flies fast through airy clouds, squinting to see a very faint image of the Hiltovian castle. Horns blown one by one on the rooftop are blasted loud. Valinor looks around, than sees a scout running up the stairs. Scout, "Lord Valinor! In intruder has been spotted in the skies, coming in very fast." Valinor turns to the scout rapidly and asks, "Identified?" Eager to please, the scout replies, "We think… it's an elf." The lords start loudly talking at once. ValInor turns to the others and commands, "Quiet!" He than turns to the scout, "What, flying?"

Valinor puts his hand out for the scout to hand him his scope. Valinor looks through the scope intensely. "A Sabonian, Sabian." The Hiltovian King states. In another blink of the eye landing from out of nowhere, surprising all of them, Sabian arrives, "King Valinor, we must talk." All of the commanders pull out their axes, as King Valinor walks right up to Sabian. Valinor says, "I am the High King of Hiltoviia." Sabian lowers his head to Valinor. A long moment goes by…Sabian raises his head.

Sabian speaks in the Hiltovoan language, "Oril sprakun Hiltovian, jan kulan winu, gonomhka kovonio." SUBTITLES FOR HILTOVIAN: I plead you fight with us for peace. In the modern tongue, not revealing he respects Sabian speaking his language of old, replies, "Modern tongue will do." Abruptly tearing himself away from Sabian, Valinor states harshly, "I don't trust outsiders. I make war and peace with whom I want, when I want."

In a sharp, scaring way, never before have words been spoken, continuing with this, "You have your ways Sabonian and 'we' have ours." Sabian figures he may rebuttal at this point, "Sabonian? As though I am so different from you. We share the same planet, the same air." Delving lower Valinor lashes out in a stone solid face, "Take it how you will."

Time is stretched out when at last the Sabonian King thinks to say, "We are people bleeding the same. And Hiltovian food, has always been to my liking." Sabian smirks though Valinor reveals none his eyes flinch. Sabian notices two of the lords smirking.

Valinor hand signals to his lords to lower their weapons, which they do with some hesitation. Valinor retorts, "Our skin is different." Valinor turns away from Sabian.

Sabian, "On the inside we are the same!" Turning away harshly, Valinor walks out of the single door on the rooftop, one of the lords, with orange skin, follows. Sabian, "Valinor wait, do you want our children to have the same struggles?!" Sabian walks fast toward the doorway. A few of the lords' step in front of the doorway, holding their axes high. Sabian, "Think of the future! Do you want your children to have the same arguments?!"

An army sits on the ground in triangle formations, with their eyes closed, and heads up toward the sky. Sabian flies overhead, landing next to Nikoli, Drusaka, Mar, Kilique, Zet, and Zutsiar by one of the campfires. Many eyes of the army look to him. Zutsiar says warmly, "Welcome back." "Valinor?" Sabian catches his breath, "He will not join us, not today. Yet I have a plan."

Turning to Kilique and Zet, Sabian asks, "I heard our spies were correct? I heard his move against Diterexitre, will be tonight." Zet and Kilique both nod to Sabian. Kilique says, "Our spies were correct?" Sabian nods to Kilique and Zet and turns to Zutsiar. Sabian, "Brother, I need you to lead the army here, as a sign to Valinor that we will not be ignored." Zutsiar nods to Sabian. "We'll show him we need to fight as one to overcome Diterexitre."

"Diterexitre sends another force to take the Stones, which I must go and help protect." The Sabonian states as Nikoli steps closer to him asking, "Alone?" Sabian nods to her. Zutsiar reaches his hand to Sabian's, shaking each other's forearms. Zutsiar, "You shouldn't go alone brother." Nikoli, "Where are 'we' going?" Sabian, "To the temple." Never before has Nikoli been so serious, about saving the world and more. Straight up into the air Sabian flies, Nikoli, Alderon, Ban, Kilique, and Mar, are lifted off of the ground in his energy trail, white, red, and blue energy trail.

CHAPTER 27

The Temple Last Stand

At the temple where the Stones of Nature are kept, actually in the forest surrounding it, Wafiroth, Rainerie, and Spairo, are running along a snowy trail with hundreds of soldiers flying and running after them. Spotting the temple's dome ceiling ahead. Wafiroth yells out mid stride, "Where are the knights?!"

Spairo points over to the side of the trail to where Drale and Shadewell, and several knights lie dead. Wafiroth glances while running. Spairo, "Ambushed after we unburied the stones!" Wafiroth, "Do you have them?!" Spairo, "Yes!" Rainerie, "Head in the temple! I'll give you cover!" Rainerie stops running, turns to face the incoming soldiers as his hands change color from ebon to green.

Wafiroth and Spairo stop, Spairo shouts, "No, we can make it together!" Rainerie turns around to Spair. Rainerie interjects, "Please, let me do this!" Wafiroth and Spairo continue running. Dozens of rocks fly over from all over the ground as Rainerie lifts his hands up... the rocks start smashing into the twisted, fearsome soldiers, deprived of the peace the afterlife would normally bring.

Spairo and Wafiroth both arrive at the door of the temple, both reaching their hands above it feeling around. Spairo, "Where is the key?" Rainerie's body and face reveal great effort as he closes his hands and makes two fists, forming many rocks into a large wall.

Spairo, "Got it!" Spairo pulls down the large key and scurries to get it in the keyhole. Wafiroth and Spairo turn when hearing a crash from Rainerie's direction. A gigantic stone lifts from on top of the wall in front of them, onto a group of soldiers. Many of the soldiers swarm around or over the wall to get bombarded with smaller rocks.

Shoving the key in the keyhole, Spairo jiggles it with all she's got to open the door swiftly. Rainerie's hands are shaking, held out in front of him as dozens of large rocks break through multiple tree branches to form the wall wider and higher. On the other side of the wall soldiers are pounding and scratching, trying to force their way through.

In the temple is a dome ceiling made mostly of stone, in the center is a circle of stain glass with chrome hatching. Directly below is a mantle to which Spairo is running. Rainerie, fatigued, runs inside. Wafiroth turns, and helps Rainerie slam the door shut. A thud echoes throughout the chamber. Granting the threesome a moment of tranquility commencing the fury of the storm the beasts bring paralleling their attack.

The rock wall falls down on the forest floor. Soldiers climb and glide over the rocks and boulders. Litulaka and Drexzulath step over the rocks on the ground, waving a fleet of winged soldiers ahead. Drexzulath raises his hands in the air. A few hundred more soldiers appear from a pink, purple and smoky black smoke and fly toward the temple.

CHAPTER 28

Diterexitre The Dark Lord

In another part of the world, inside one of the caves of the tremendous fortress, Diterexitre closes his eyes while sitting in his throne. An ebon energy drifts out of Vilanowa, lying still on the ground near the throne, and is absorbed into Diterexitre.

Disappearing into thin air, Diterexitre proceeds into the shadows of one of the corners of the room. Sorg enters the same room, looks to Vilanowa, as his eyes scroll up to focus on the other presence in the room, believing another is near.

The mentor to the apprentice gazes, and upon closer inspection of Vilanowa he sees the transfer of energy taking place. Further probing, grants him to realize that the generals lying on the stone slated floor were being used to build his apprentice stronger. Sorg, "Diterexitre?"

Knowing he's there now. He steps past the throne and to the sill of the single small circular window. A tiny droplet like material of black ooze nears his long nailed, talon lengthy fingers as he places them both on the cold stone sill.

Diterexitre's voice is heard yet when Sorg looks here and there and soon everywhere in the room it dawns on him that his apprentice is invisible. Shockingly Sorg hears the voice of Diterexitre with a raspier tone, "I sense fear, ironic, and that one who thrives on fear in others now associates to it in a different way."

"What trick are you playing at?" Sorg says transforming to his more elf like appearance than his other creature form. The morph angers Diterexitre more so, just thinking that Sorg watched as he scrambled helplessly to save his parents. Surely he could have swayed down to lend a hand in all his power, and Diterexitre answers "No trick, like the one on me, eh, we shall see?" Diterexitre snickers.

"What are you talking about?" Sorg says, trying his best to not appear a liar. Knowing full well that he could feel the immense power surging through Ditetexitre, may even surpass his own now. "On the contrary ... This is a serious game." Diterexitre says now more stern than he ever has spoken to Sorg. Sorg finds Diterexitre rebuilding himself, standing in front of his throne now from out of thin air, both of his hands swirling in pink, purple, and black energy.

"There is more to what happened that you don't understand!" Sorg shouts.

Diterexitre, stunned now, overwhelmed with curiosity, lowers his hands, "For your sake, this best not be a lie." In a pouring out of words, Sorg replies, "It's not, you see your mother and father were also my apprentices, yet you were the one all along who held my attention, the one I sought to aid however I could. I never wanted them to die. I... did all I..."

"Wrong answer, you watched them die!" Diterexitre's very voice shatters the glass on the one window. Raising his hands, now arms above his head as a flood of gas comes over Sorg. Rendering him helpless despite his magic pouring out of his hands. Diterexitre's rage overwhelms him. Sorg lies still on the ground as the Diterexitre's magic seeps into him. "You are nothing more than a stain removed."

A commander, in full plate mail armor walks in. The commander speaks in angry type voice, one seeking to find what plain of existence she belongs to, the living or the none, and says, "The Hiltovian army approaches lord Diterexitre." "I knew they would. See to it." Diterexitre says, as the commander bows and exits. Diterexitre closes his eyes for a few beats and takes a long, deep breath, when he reopens them a whirlwind of smoke forms into a cocoon like sphere in front of him.

Diterexitre, "All that you could you say? My mother and father were killed. Perhaps you were even the reason. You shall feel what I've learned, adrift, in pain, casted away by my people thanks to your efforts." Diterexitre creates a large semi solid and semi gaseous ebon battle- ax in his hands. Diterexitre strikes Sorg and Sorg screams out.

CHAPTER 29

The Sabonian Temple Last Stand

An ebon battle- ax, semi solid and semi gaseous, forms into Lituluka's and Drexzulath's hands, much to their surprise. Drexzulath, "Master?" Diterexitre's voice pops into Drexzulath's head, "Yes Drexzulath." Hundreds of soldiers, once elves, humans, or dwarves, swarm over the temple. Inside the temple, Wafiroth, Spairo, and Rainerie run up to the mantel and place the two Stones of Nature on it.

Scratching and smashing sounds ricochet from outside through the ceiling dome as soldiers flood inside. Drexzulath looks up and sees Sabian flying overhead with the others. The general of a soulless army commands, "To the skies!" Hundreds of soldiers fly off toward Sabian. They spray an ebon substance from their mouths and hands. From the hand that Sabian has forward, emanates a bright white, red, and blue energy at the soldiers.

Hundreds of soldiers are swarming into the gigantic temple. Spairo, "We must send the stones away!" All three wizards place their hands' atop of the stones yet Wafiroth sees the soldiers nearing. Spairo, "One of us has to hold them off!" Rainerie shouts, "It takes all of us to cast the stones!" Wafiroth, "You'll have to try!"

The elements serve us as we serve them as Wafiroth pulls out his staff from under his cloak and from it a large wall of water disperses at the soldiers. Many soldiers slam into the water as it pushes them back in a drowning wave. Soldiers spray an- ebon ooze and punch and scrape at the wall. The holes they make become instantly filled with a very lively water. Spairo and Rainerie shout, "Alrantiogoth, Ranwovenal!"

Outside the old stone temple Sabian, Nikoli, Alderon, Ban, Kilique, and Mar land and look all around. A hundred lying on the ground are a cinder, with traces of Sabian's magic dissolving from their bodies. Drexzulath and dozens of soldiers attack. Sabian, "They must be inside the temple. Can you hold them off?" He turns to the others. Alderon, "Go!"

With lighting like speed Sabian sprints toward Lituluka, pounding at the temple door. Drexzulath teleports in front of Sabian and swings his battle-ax in at him, spreading a whirling wind that surrounds them, taking them into the air. Lituluka smashes the door with the ax, causing a hole and ooze to eat at the door.

The others insisting on coming with Sabian are surrounded. They do their best shooting arrows and swinging their bladed weapons to keep squadron at bay. Alderon, "We must get to the temple door!" Sabian and Drexzulath fly in and out of clouds, wrestling in a whirl- wind of magic.

Inside the temple a few of the soldiers blow ooze into one area of the wall of water, creating a hole for a few dozen to fly through. Wafiroth lowers his staff. Water ceases to come out of it as he staggers to keep posture. The soldiers are nearing.

Lituluka crashes the door open and runs in with dozens of soldiers. Lituluka hears a battle cry from behind him, seeing Alderon, Nikoli, and Ban, running in as well. Lituluka raises his battle-ax and a wave of the ebon ooze heads toward them. They dive out of the way yet crash on the ground, all but Nikoli regaining herself.

Right outside the temple door, armed with an ax and shield, Kilique steps back to back with Mar, holding a halberd. Mar, "We've got to help them!" Kilique, "We are!" Kilique and Mar run and strike down six soldiers running inside Nikoli, Ban, and Alderon.

Rainerie turns from the stones to Lituluka walking toward him. Rainerie kneels on the ground then places both palms against the stone floor. Rainerie, "Roots arise!"

Tiny roots come through the floor, grabbing the legs of Lituluka. He breaks them off and keeps coming.

Spairo stands over the pedestal. A flock of soldiers fly at her. She raises both of her hands over her head creating a sparkling white sphere over her and the mantle. Spairo, "Wafirs hurt Rainerie!" Rainerie looks over shoulder, seeing soldiers swarming everywhere. Spairo orders, "Rainerie grab Wafiroth and get in here!"

In the swiftest of dashes Rainerie can he heads to Wafiroth, an old friend of his, who is falling to his knees. He grabs Wafiroth's waist and runs for the sphere. Rainerie is only half way in the sphere when Lituluka grabs his leg and yanks it.

Screaming out Rainerie's leg slips out of Lituluka's grip. Spairo is concentrating hard to keep the sphere up. Lituluka crashes his battle-ax against the sphere, causing a large crack. Spairo, "Come to the stones!" Spairo and Rainerie help Wafiroth stand up as a lot of blood drips from their wounds.

"Kill them!" Litulaka commands soldiers to fly through the crack in the sphere as he tried to pull his ax out of it. Biting and gnawing away at Wafiroth, Spairo and Rainerie, the soldiers flood into the sphere. In dire agony Spairo and Rainerie place one of their hands on the stones, while their other hand fights off the soldiers. Rainerie grabs one of Wafiroth's hands and pulls it up to the stones, yet a few soldiers tear into him. Rainerie, "Agh!!!"

Solid steel in the form of a battle- axe comes crashing down at Rainerie's backside. Though the blades wielder is surprised it hits into a thing of hot energy like a foam shield, one red, white, and blue. The ax does not meet whom it was intended to.

Spairo gets woozy and the sphere fades with the remains of her strength. A shinning red, white, and blue sword is shoved through Lituluka's back... Lituluka falls. The soldiers scatter. Spairo, Wafiroth, and Rainerie see Sabian holding the sword. "Send the stones away!" The High Elf King orders. Spairo, Wafiroth, and Rainerie shout in synchrony, "Alrantiogoth, Ranwovenall...Sargorn!" Nikoli, Alderon, Ban, Kilique, and Mar run into the temple. A flashing light strikes as the two stones disappear. Outside of the temple hundreds of soldiers are struck with the red, white, and blue energy, disintegrating them. Drexzulath, struck with the same energy cringes and disappears.

CHAPTER 30

The War Goes On

Elsewhere at the mountain canyon, Zutsiar, Kulundra, Drusaka, and Tolomal, sit on steeds in front of the army. Snow falls on them as well as the fire pits they have made. They raise their attention to distant war horns and yelling. Zutsiar shouts out, "Sound the charge!" Drusaka and Tolomol blow horns as well.

At Diterexitre's castle Valinor accompanied by his lords are on Dragon Horses, a breed of both a smaller dragons features and stallions, in the middle of thousands of their knights. The Hiltovian army is knee- deep fighting tens of thousands of darkened soldiers, each more horrid than the next. Snow is all around them. A Hiltovian general, with red skin and sand colored armor pulls on the reigns of his brown dragon horse…making it roar to intimate the engaging them.

General, "We have to fall back my King!" Valinor refuses, "No! Order the others!" On a nearby hill stepping out from the gloomy painted shadows, emanating a massive ebon energy Diterexitre stirs. Casting his full strength outward to strike Valinor. Valinor shrieks, "Ughh!" The General grabs his horn around his shoulder and blows.

The Sabonian and Alphinian army charge over hills. Valinor gives a snicker when seeing the other cultures of kind. Valinor is covered in blood, seeing his General, a few commanders, and many Hiltovians lying on the ground.

A loud rumble shakes the ground, giving pause to all on the battle- field. Caladar, a giant Dragon Elf, about twenty feet tall, wearing some armor and not much else, appears from out of nowhere in the middle of the battle- field. The giant loudly claps his hands together. Caladar, "Away!" An enormous, shockwave spreads out of Caladar's hands. Within seconds all those on the battlefield disappear into thin air.

In the lands of the Mountains of the dwarves, a stocky Mountain Dwarf wearing rags and a few furs treads with determination, plowing in thick snow. He has frost along a thick white beard, and long, raggedy gray hair. Inside the Mountain Dwarves cave four Mountain Dwarf knights in stone armor and thick furs stand by a cave entrance lit by four torches. They hear footsteps. They pull their weapons out, one a spear, one an ax, one a sword, and the last a bow and arrow.

Outside the Mountain Dwarf walks along a snowy path, one sparkling as tiny crystals, stops for a moment, and takes a deep sniff. The dwarf walks out from behind a mountain into plain sight of the knights. The lone dwarf raises his hand up, palm out and fingers straight up, than makes a fist. The Mountain Dwarf holding a sword raises his hand, palm out, than makes a fist. Dwarven knight, "My Lord?" The knights lower their weapons.

Within the Dwarven Mountain King, Narok, has a long beard, long brown and white hair, wears gray and tan cotton robes, and has a stone helmet with two horns on his lap. He sits in a throne made of stone, laced with gold. His head is low.

Mountain Dwarf knights in stone armor are scattered throughout the caves chambers, each standing near a torch. Narok all of a sudden lifts his head up, stands up, taking a step away from his throne. The dwarf from outside limps in through the arched stone doorway, "Karok, brother!" Karok, "Aye, I'm home." Narok and Karok hug. The guards lower their weapons and kneel.

Along the ocean strip during broad daylight, Sabian, Nikoli, Zutsiar, and Kulundra stand together near the water. Mountains are in the distance behind them. Nikoli speaks as a a natural leader, wise, brave, and comfortingly, "Everyone?" Zutsiar replies in the most confused state he had experienced, "We all appeared here, Diterexitre, the Hiltovians, were gone."

Sabian says, "Perhaps saving many, for now." Zutsiar, "So brother, what's this surprise you mentioned?" Sabian spreads his arms out wide. Sabian, "Trenta, our kingdom, the largest city the world has ever known. We are going to build it here." The four of them smile at each other. Kulundra says, "If I may, is this the wisest time?" Sabian glances to Nikoli, who answers, "The people need more than a fight to keep them going, more to keep them feeling alive. We will be rebuilding the city of old Badella, into something people can feel will bring them hope, other than a sword in their hand." They nod to her agreeing.

A pyramid shape structure begins taking shape, standing in the center of the huge construction sight. Sabian hammers a nail into a 4x4 that connects to a plank of wood. He hears hammering in the distance and looks out over the sight; millions are working: pulling, lifting, and hoisting large pieces of wood and stone.

In a thin white cloud, sheltering her from being witnessed by others, Asate appears behind Sabian, startling him a bit. Sabian says half kiddingly, "Sorceress, you have a way of surprising me." Asate, that is my name Sabian. The giant who ended the battle is name Caladar, one of the last guardians of another world, an ally to the late Quinatal, he believes in you as well, though no one can prevent the war to come much longer. We will need Hiltovia to unite." Sabian nods agreeably, "Yet how can..." Before he has a chance to finish she is gone with the wind.

CHAPTER 31

A Survivors Path

In a throne made of bones, further content than he has ever been, Diterexitre sits, seemingly more powerful than ever. Cao, in the shape of a few inches tall, is sitting on his shoulder. Diterexitre says in a voice that would make the dead tremble, "The Spell of Ages took much, now it is time to take whatever I can from them…whatever they hold most dear, indeed, shall be mine!" His last words echo so much so that the throne, the surroundings include shake, enough to send Cao flying from his shoulder, morphing to a small dragon like bat form flying out of the one window in the labyrinth.

Dusk by a waterfall close to the Dark Lord's dungeon, yet free of most of its prisoners of late. Caladar stands under water, rubbing water over his face. He hears a rumbling noise advancing before it's too late a tremendous pink, purple, and black cloud is upon him, one percolating with lighting. Diterexitre walks out from behind Caladar.

The giant lies on the rocky ground, ooze covers him as the cloud dissipates to Diterexitre waving his hand aside. Cao is standing proudly on top of the giant's chest, admiring his unconscious state. Diterexitre places his hands on his hips, flourishing in his victory over the great foreign giant, "Wise wizards, casting the Stones Of Nature so far, though too bad their peace keeper, is all mine." Diterexitre laughs wickedly, loud so much so birds nearby filter from the comfort of the trees to the sky.

Placing both of his hands in front of him, spreading the oily ooze substance via his fingertips. Cao flies up from the ground and onto Diterexitre's shoulder as the ooze seeps into the ground around them. Diterexitre, "To find the

Stones of Nature I must plunge into the very heart of the world." Covered in the ooze, Caladar struggles to open his eyes, lying somewhat twenty feet behind them. Caladar struggles to break free. Cao stirs, hearing Caladar, in an attempt to call out she says, "Diterexitre?"

"Not now Cao!" Diterexitre sarcastically dismisses her continuing with his plan. Caladar pulls one of his arms out of the ooze; then pulls most of the ooze off of his face. Caladar says, "You...must...stop!" Caladar frees his other arm. Diterexitre pauses.

Cao flies up in the air frantically, screeching loudly, growing into a large purple and black dragon. Diterexitre steps to Caladar, who is groggily standing up. A fury comes over Diterexitre, his hands glow in gloomy tones. Caladar slaps his hands together, sending a shock wave out.

Diterexitre releases a conglomerate of magic from his hands that just barely deflect the shock wave before knocking him over. An explosion occurs, Cao, hovering in the sky, flies higher to avoid it. Cao grows more than ten times, altering to look more like a black dragon, than descends toward Caladar. Screaming out at the top of his lungs while pouring on all that he can, utterly dissolving Caladar in a black flame.

CHAPTER 32

Foreign Alliances

In the Mountain Dwarves Kings' chamber, Narok and Karok sit on two wooden chairs at a stone table by a roaring fire- place. Fine silver wear, discarded food on silver plates, and a few candles are atop of the table. Narok, "You say it was a Sabonian elf who saved you." Karok nods. Narok, "I think we shall be thanking the Sabonians, from this day to the end.

CHAPTER 33

Dark Lord and a Changling

In the forest named Frondrok, among weeping willow trees, gigantic pine trees, neighbors a bright yellow-bluish river. Despite the storm that brews overhead Sabian thinks of the way his home was. These days it is merely a graveyard. Diterexitre saw to that. Thick, gray clouds sculpted by a puppet master of sorts paint the sky. Dressing trees, the sandy beach, the field, and the river lives the plague appearing as oil, nearing too close for comfort.

CHAPTER 34

Trenta Forming

Main Square, standing here and there are groups of Sabonian, Alphinian, and one or two Hiltovian villagers. They look to Drusaka and Feltak who are standing in front of them.

A rustic, Alphinian villager asks, "What of this darkness? It's in the sky, the rivers, and soil." A mix of chatter rises as the villager rubs his forehead. A Sabonian villager joins in, "How are we to farm, how are we to eat? My children are scared." Drusaka raises his hand and says to all around, "We only need to stay together." Feltak begins to talk indiscreetly as she approaches a few villagers in the front row. Wafiroth, Rainerie, and Spairo, in the back, lower their hoods. Rainerie closes his eyes for a long moment, and reopens them in realization of something.

CHAPTER 35

The Dark Lord On The Move

On the outside of Diterexitre's castle wall Caladar is unconscious, his body is wrapped in a cocoon of the black ooze. A series of metal brackets and chains pin him up against one of the castle's stone- walls.

CHAPTER 36

Trenta's Rising

Sunrise woke on a long, cobbled stone, road passes through two sets of gates. The road leads from the forest in the south to the city. The inner gate, made of stone, and several feet thick, never mind a hundred feet tall. As the outer wall this one circles the castle. Thousands of shops and village homes are in the center of the inner gate, as is a stone draw- bridge, a few feet thick.

A grass field is what lies behind the outer wall. Located on both gates are large stone towers under construction. Thousands of elves and hundreds of speed wagon are being used to transport stone, wood, and other material. Speed Wagons: machines varying in size from an average tank to nearly ten times that, made up of wood, and controlled by a series of levers, and a driver are varying in design though for the most part resemble a partially open train.

Thousands of students ranging in age from teenagers to seniors, Sabonians, Alphinians, and a few Hiltovians, are standing on a lawn in front of Feltak and Drusaka. Drusaka walks several paces over to the students, "Now than, we are ready to begin!" Feltak looks to thousands that have gathered closer toward to her. She waves her hand in a circular motion. Feltak, "Studying magic, you must be in tune with nature and especially the power we feel from the sun rising!" Suddenly one of Fetlak's hands has flame around it.

The entire group mimics Feltak, though nobody has a flame around their hand. Vi, a teenage Sabonian elf with ebon skin and brown robes, forms a steady red flame around both hands. Everyone around him is shocked. Feltak sees Vi and is shocked. The flame around Feltak's hand fades as she walks towards Vi. He is a Sabonian with skin a bit ivory yet beige as a human, short brown hair, wearing a brown leather shirt, cotton pants, and leather shoes. "Excellent. Excellent!" Feltak says above the Indistinct chatter among the students. Feltak, "What is your name?" Vi replies, "Vi." Feltak smirks to Vi. Feltak, "Everyone, your squad leader is Vi!"

Later that day in Trenta, the city, between a beach coast and a mountain range, in the middle of a forest with trees of various color. Hundreds of Sabonia workers with hammers, shovels, and such are at it like there's no tomorrow. Thousands of villagers are among shops, stands, and homes. Mean while inside the High Council chamber Feltak, Drusaka, Wafiroth, Spairo, Mar, and Rainerie, sitting around a candle lit table. Feltak, "My magic, I feel it slipping away, along with other things." Drusaka and the others nod in agreement. Spairo, "A sign that the Stones of Nature are weakening with their separation."

Jumping in, though calmly, Mar adds, "I thought when they were casted out we would be better off?" Feltak turns to Mar, "We are. If Diterexitre ceased them there it would have been a quick end to us all." She says to the Alphinian Prince, glancing to Spairo who nods to her saying, "We do know one of the stones is close, and Sabian must find it." Kilique asks, "And the other stone?" Wafiroth relies in short, fondling his short beard, "Far away." Rainerie, "But not safe."

The others look to Rainerie, growing more fearful. Most of them lower their heads for an instant yet on as if on que Sabian and Nikoli enter. Mar is first to stand up, than steps towards Sabian, the others go to stand as well, yet the King raises his hands, "Please there is no need, sit." The group remains seated than when Mar says to Sabian. Taking another step toward he and the Queen, "My father...I, would like you to have this."

Sabian and the others are shocked. Mar begins to unstrap the trident strapped to his back- side. Raising his hands, and stepping right up to Mar, reading him as close as he can... Gaining a feeling from his expressions that it saddens the Prince to part with. "Wait, please my friend. I ask only this. Keep it, your father honored me. Do the same by holding onto that, which is the Alphinian, your trident of the sea." Mar hesitates, Sabian stares to him sincerely and with hopeful eyes. "I understand." Mar nods to him.

Within the walls of the bedroom of Nikoli and Sabian they catch what down time they can before the break of day. Sitting on the side of their bed, hugging each other tighter and tighter. Behind them the door is ajar. Sabian strongly, in a concerned tone says, "In the days of yesterday, with the fiber that it is the core of my being, I have fell short in imagination dreaming of a lady so spiritually strong in all the ways that would define an angel. Your eyes are as two stars with the most precious of crystals in the center. When I hug you I can feel lightening pulsing in my body, new sparks of life in all of its glory, warmth, and happiness."

A heavy rainfall begins outside, heard by the window open a quarter. Together, they get up from the bed to walk to the window. Thunder and lightening shrieks thoughtout the clouds. Concerned expressions form on their faces, "Diterexitres gained power." Sabian says. Nikoli, "I feel it too. Be careful." Sabian, "I will." Nikoli and Sabian hug each other again.

In the long hallway outside of the King and Queen's chamber Rainerie is standing outside when he turns away, quietly walking down the hallway. Rainerie, "I will help you. I, like so many, believe we owe you for answering a world in need."

A few days later under the light of the sun a camp in the middle of Trenta's Forest, under a glaring moon, Sabian, Zutsiar, Alderon, and Ban sit on boulders around a campfire. Ban is sharpening his ax with a stone while Zutsiar and Alderon are eating corn on the cob.

Roaring is the campfire in the middle of a clearing of pine trees. Traces of the black ooze are in the distance, on the ground around them. Sabian is writing on a scroll when he stops, stares at a large tree, and smirks at seeing the tree start as one and than split into two barks. He embarks down memory lane to years ago.

As a teenager, standing on a village street he sees a Sabonian news agent, barely in his twenties, with pale gray skin, holding a scroll in his hand, and a sac in the other. Walking down the street toward a group of Sabonian villagers he hears something that will forever change his life. The newsagent shouts, "Diterexitres terror! Village scouts report the same! Read about it here!" Villagers are terrified, vividly lit by torches around the cobbled stone village street. Flames which just all go out in a swift sweep of a strong southern gust.

Among the warmth of a fireplace burning wood away throughout the night, in his old bedroom when he was a boy. His parents, Darion and Holera are standing in the door- way looking at him sitting on the bed looking out the window. His mother Holera, wearing a cotton shirt and pants, approaches him with sincerity, asking, "What is it son?"

He replies, "I can't sleep mom, and no one can explain these things that are happening to me, and around the village." Darion and Holera, in their pajamas, and wool robes over them, walk in the bedroom to sit down beside their son, no more than twenty.

Darion, his father, fairly clean cut and as charismatic as his mother asks, "Is that what's troubling you, or is it the newspapers?" Sabian takes a deep breath and shakes his head. Sabian, "No, I mean yes, that's nerve wrecking, but its something else. I, I can't find, anyone." His father continues, "Son, you are special, and there's bound to be somebody like you, with your gifts..." "That's not what I mean, someone to love." Sabian, nervous a bit and embarrassed as well takes a deep sign. "When the time is right, you will, you will see." His mother says. They go to get up from beside him, when his father says furthermore, "In the meantime, we will be with you, always my sons."

Back to the present time, his emotional eyes tear away from the fire pit upon hearing his brother call to him. Echoing as he slowly, though surely comes to the moment. Sabian, further content than the norm of late, opens his eyes and stares at a bright group of stars. Zutsiar walks over to Sabian.

Zutsiar says, "Brother? Were you sleeping?" Replying to his slightly older brother, Sabian says calmly, "I must have drifted off there down memory lane, thinking about mom and dad." Zutsiar says most caringly, smiling, "That's good. I think you need to eat. I've been saving this sweet fish." Zutsiar reaches into his bag, hanging off a tree branch. He pulls out a silver flask of wine and a foot long package.

"My closest friends, together." Sabian says coming to. Ban comically replies, "Your only friends." The four of them laugh. Alderon chuckling away joins in by stating, "And one of them is your brother." Ban, Zutsiar, and Sabian look at Alderon stunned, and than laugh. Sabian smiles contributing, "I haven't heard you make a joke in a long time Alderon." They all, except Sabian take a sip from their cups that put his aside. "Not drinking." Asks his brother. "Giving it up brother." Everyone nods to him with a mix of respect and slight surprise. Alderon pats Sabian on the back, "Good for you." The four of them watch the flame become brighter from a gust of wind.

Sometime later, Ban and Zutsiar are awake, laughing and drinking in front of a dim fire. Sabian and Alderon are asleep, and Sabian's cup he left full a top the boulder is empty. Ban drops his mug on a stone, partially buried in the ground, it shatters in pieces. Sabian wakes up. Sabian. "All right you two." Ban and Zutsiar look at each other, trying to stop from laughing. Ban, "Shh."

Zutsiar, "Me, you shh." Ban, "Mesho? Who's that?" Zutsiar and Ban laugh. Sabian, "Quiet." Sabian gives an annoyed gaze to them. Ban looks around the forest, than to Zutsiar. Ban, "Hey Zutsiar?" Ban, "Did you hear that?" Firmly, Zutsiar, "No." Ban, "Neither did I!" They look at each other seriously then burst out in hysterical laughter. Sabian throws off his blanket, springing up like a rake's blade being stepped on from lying on the ground, shouting, "Will you two shut up!!"

Later that night, when things had settled under a full moon, Sabian, Zutsiar, Ban, and Alderon fall asleep. Morning dawns, taking its time as if to give the warriors born an extra long break from the hardships they have faced. With it the foursome makes their next move. Zutsiar, "Brother, wake up." Zutsiar says. Alderon with his shorter, bearded friend, Ban, are packing their backpacks with their weapons, torches, and empty bottles. Soloed out, Sabian hears a humming noise, drawing away. Zutsiar, "What is it?"

Convinced the sound is apparent, Sabian asks quite questioningly, "Don't you hear it?" Sabian grabs his backpack than runs into the thick forest. Inside of a cave he goes. Companions trailing behind his feather light foot steps.

Glancing to Zutsiar, Ban asks, "How long are we going keep this up?" Shaking his head offering no answers Zutsiar shrugs his shoulders. Seconds after he does whisper, "For as long as it takes." Alderon and Sabian walk carefully in between flame spewing out of the floor and ceiling as though a lava field pulses throughout. They side step the fire then both look up, spotting a clearing in the tunnel.

Alderon missteps, extremely close to the flame… Sabian grabs Alderon's arm, pulling him to safety. Sabian, "We've got to stick together." Alderon sighs in relief. Ban and Zutsiar approach the fiery area. Ban, "Fire, I hate fire." Zutsiar shakes his head to Sabian, who rolls his eyes and smiles to his brother.

In the open woods of the forest birds are chirping in sweet song. Garbug and Galtrit, two Mountain Dwarf knights, wearing stone plate armor, are walking down a trail when they halt in their tracks. Asate, the Dwelven sorceress, is several paces behind them.

Wal, a Dragon-Cat, half tiger, half dragon, four feet off the ground, with tan fur and black stripes, closely tails behind her. Garbug whistles and the others stop.

Galtrit hand signals to Asate she stops walking up the trail and closes her eyes. Rustling noises from up ahead startle the birds off of the tree-tops. Wal starts sniffing up ahead. Garbug quietly unsheathes his sword. Galtrit readies his bow. Garbug spots movement of a long black tail in the thick brush ahead. Garbug whispers, "Split up." Galtrit and Garbug hesitate as Asate, hovers past them. Asate reaches a clearing, witnessing Cao as a black dragon, licking a wound.

Asate, "You are not of this world. "Why are you on Earth?" Cao looks to her caught off guard, her tongue hanging out still. Cao answers the sorceress,

"I serve the Dark Lord, wherever he travels." Sharply Asate responds with this" His magic keeps this world in danger. Using too much from the cosmos is deadly." Cao rebuttals, "As does the elf who leads you."

Asate, "He only does so because he must. Even your master Diterexitre knows that elven magic creates and heals, as light does, and that of darkness destroys." Cao stands up, higher than twenty feet.

Asate, "Will you let us go by in peace?" Cao sniffs around the area, "I cannot!" Cao breaths' a blackish green fire at her. Asate puts both of her arms over her head and a thin yellow cylindrical shield forms over both of her hands, shouting, "Falondrol Urik!"

Galtrit and Garbug jump out of the bushes. Wal sweeps down, breaking thru branches, swinging his paw and slashing Cao. Cao screeches. The discus shaped shield spins round dispersing most of the flame up in the air.

Elsewhere, in The Lost Tree Field, Sabian, Zutsiar, Alderon, and Ban walk out of the cave way, amazed to see a vast field of giant trees in front of them, many of which are covered in the black ooze. Zutsiar, "I don't believe this place is on any maps." Zutsiar and Ban look back, as they step further away from the cave.

"The stone must be here somewhere. Yet the humming is faint now." Sabian says, "Let's split up." Sabian, Alderon, Zutsiar, and Ban walk away from each other and head further into the thickening trees. The moon- lights up the forest. Sabian is walking alone, the others hundreds of feet apart searching for clues to one of The Stones of Natures whereabouts. He looks up to the sky, noticing a single bright beam of starlight shining downward in front of him.

He traces the beam to a single tree in the distance. Sabian hurriedly walks toward that tree. He notices that the trees near that one are vibrant with green, blue, and pink leaves. Sabian, "Is this my imagination? Now there's no trace, and I'm talking to myself."

A thing pierces his pointy ivory ears, hearing the humming louder than before. He flies off fast above the ground toward the tree. Rainerie"s voice say, "You are given this stone by the right of one it's guardians." He stops flying Sabian directly in front of that particular tree with the beam, "Rainerie is that you? Are you here?" Sabian looks all around, seeing nothing. He touches the tree and his hand goes through it. He feels something when pulling his hand back out. Grabbing onto it, he fully pulls his arm out, opening his palm. A Stone of Nature is revealed, swirling with green and brown hues.

A wave of darkness comes over the forest, covering it completely. The wind blows hard. The stone flies out of Sabian's hand. "No! I'll not let you have it!" A red, blue, and white light bursts out of Sabian's hand as he flies toward the stone. With all the might ascending from the creators of this world he grabs onto it. Zutsiar runs over and leaps at Sabian though Sabian disappears just before he can grab him. Zutsiar smacks onto the ground shouting to whatever twisted source that has ensnared his younger, "Don't take him! Dammit!"

Alderon and Ban come running over to Zutsiar's side. Ban, "What's going on Zutsiar?!" Alderon, "Diterexitre, he's got Sabian! We have to warn the Council!" Zutsiar lifts his head up to the sky distressed and screams "Sabian?! This is madness! What is happening to this world. Zutsiar up on his knees, barely feeling able to stand says.

Watery eyed, "Alderon, how can we continue this fight?" Stepping beside Zutsiar, placing his hand on his shoulder, Alderon says, "Because, we must fight for those who cannot, for our children and theirs, peace must not be given up on." Zutsiar knowing the wisdom of Alderon's words yet not absorbed in entirety says, "Can it though, will there not always be a fight? An injustice?" Ban steps over to Zutsiar's other side, placing his own, slightly stubby hand on his other shoulder, contributing, and "All the more reason to spread the word to everyone… 'everywhere,' that unions build the world fairly, not prejudices." They nod to each other, helping Zutsiar stand once more.

CHAPTER 37

Diterexitre's Strike

In a red and purple sky, a light forms twenty feet above the ground. Sabian falls from the light with the stone in his hands, crashing on the ground. The light from the stone dims. A strong wind carries a cyclone of rubble and dust at Sabian. He squints, shielding his eyes with his arm. When the dust settles, Diterexitre appears in front of him, raising his hand up in the air. He and Sabian vanish in a whirl of smoke, purple, pink, and charcoal.

Diterexitre reappears. Sabian is shocked to see Galtrit, Garbug, and Asate, chained up against the castle wall, covered in the oil colored ooze. There are chains over their arms, hands, legs and feet. "Give me the stone and I will let you leave, alive!" Diterexitre shouts. Sabian replies firmly, trying hard to keep all his wit about him, "What do you want with it?" Diterexitre screams out, "You could not understand, in your perfect world! I seek revenge! For what has been taken from me!"

The High King says back, looking possible death in the eyes as a bull racing through a thunderstorm, "I cannot understand?! I have been on my hands and knees begging for all of the world, fighting for equality, for peace for all, for freedom!" Diterexitre hesitates for what could seem as a stretched out moment before shaking his head no.

A worn, half scarred finger of Diterexitre points to the far corner of the castle where Asate, Garbug, and Galtrit are chained to the wall, lifeless. Diterexitre states with an eerie confidence, "More are coming, for what you have done, taking those souls I meant to free!" Sabian rebuttals, "You mean the prisoners you were holding? You had no intention of freeing them, did you?"

So angrily so, clenching his teeth, about all he has lost, Diterexitre possessed in an uncanny way as the root of all that is not good is bound to his soul, "They would have evolved into my army!" Refusing to agree when someone's free will is taken away Sabian shouts, "No!" Sabian angers as a thin beam of red, blue and white energy comes out from his hands. Diterexitre spreads an ebon light from his hand's that meets Sabian's. Cao, as a large shadow toned dragon, flies over the roof as monstrous bat dwindling between the balances of the world.

CHAPTER 38

The Missing King

A misty rain, leaning from one side, taps onto a dimly lit tavern's wooden roof in the middle of a forest clearing. A handful of windows let's the music, singing, and chimney smoke out into the forest abroad. Alderon, Zutisar, and Ban walk out of the forest and in front of the tavern, near a glass- encased lit lantern.

The lantern hangs from an old post that has a sign hanging two hooks that says 'Tavern Of The Pines'. Reading the sign, Alderon says, "Hmph, Tavern Of The Pines, never heard of it." They follow the path to the main door. In the bathroom, a tremendously tall Hiltovian elf, with red skin stumbles to a urinal. He leans on a long mace beside him. Zutsiar enters the bathroom, walks to a urinal near the Hiltovian.

The Hiltovian looks Zutsiar up and down while smiling at him in a sarcastic way. Zutsiar, "Have a problem?" Rationalization of question leads the Hiltovian to spit on Zutsiar's neck and face, laughing at the whole thing.

Zutsiar's hand forms a tight fist as the Hiltovian walks away. Zutsiar walks up behind the elf, Zutsiar, "You owe me an apology." The Hiltovian laughs again, than appears serious as he clenches both of his red skinned fists. Hiltovian, "For what?"

Zutsiar's gloved hand wipes the spit from his face, the Hiltovian says, "I didn't 'even' see you." Zutsiar shakes his head to gesture 'no'. The Hiltovian draws a long, curved dagger than swings it at Zutsiar. Zutsiar jumps beside the Hiltovian, punching him out cold with one strong hit.

A band of four Alphinian Elves play a jazzy, funky, instrumental song that dozens of elves, of various size, shape, and style, are dancing their hearts out to. Alderon and Ban sit silently. Zutsiar comes out of the bathroom and walks over to Alderon and Ban. Zutsiar, "There's trouble here. We should go." Zutsiar, Alderon, and Ban get up and head for a door in a shady corner. Alderon and Zutsiar indiscreetly talk.

Under an awning lit by torches the King's brother and his two closest friends stand, the rain falls near them, pitter and pattering away as they look around nervously. Zutsiar at lasts says, "He was just 'sooo' arrogant." Zutsiar shakes his head back and forth. Alderon, "Zutsiar, if you believe in your brother's cause for peace you will have to choose your fights more carefully." Zutsiar lowers his head in shame. Alderon puts his hand on Zutsiar's shoulder. An uplifting squawk alerts their attention to Driona flying down onto Zutsiar's shoulder. Zutsiar, "Driona, fly fast, tell the Queen Sabian is missing." Driona flies off into the sky.

While back at Diterexitre's castle Sabian struggles to keep two thick beams of red, blue and white energy coming from out of his hands as if he can control fire water and the air itself. Up standing still against an equally exhausted foe. After a series of rays a black light comes from Diterexitre's hands and at the same time Cao's mouth, as if they are merged their spells destined at each other's throats. With all his will Sabian can barely hold on to fight, his knees buckle even as he forces his back straight. Giving all the intensity he can summon, feeling the weights world on his shoulders.

From out of thin air, as a sign that friendship, and good deeds being rewarded, Narok and Karok fly on a large brown and red dragon as fast as a cheetah can run. A screech from the dragon raises the eyebrows of those below. A split second later a blast of red flame comes forth from the dwarves reptilian ally, the size of a wagon. Cao and Diterexitre by the skin of their teeth, dive out of the way the spewing hot flame. Narok pulls on the reigns and the dragon dives down. Karok grabs Sabian, pulling him up on their saddle with his large arm's as the hero is ready to collapse like a ton of bricks.

In a rushing gliding way they fly over to Asate, Garbug, and Galtrit yet see, most unfortunately Narok says mournfully, "No signs of life." Each of them nearly as much as the other wishes more than anything to wipe them selves clean of the nauseating smell of the nightmares endowed on the poor souls held under DIterexitre's cruel hand. Burning of smoldering bodies lingers in the foul air, ones easy for him to abduct. To keep imprisoned while he drained their essences into his own.

Narok wears gold full plate battle armor, and Karok, wears full plate black armor. Karok shouts out, "I won't leave them in this forsaken place!" jumping down, revealing a battle- ax. "There is no time!" Narok shouts, witnessing Diterextire and his dragon regain themselves. Karok ignores his brother, fighting the flashbacks of once being a prisoner here, smashing the chains and stone blocks that hold their hands and feet.

A sight of horror in the noble who have sacrificed their own lives for the betterment of others, Galtrit, Garbug, and Asate are beat up and scratched, they collapse once cut free. Narok uses his massive arms to catch them just before they hit the ground. Karok carries them to the dragon than Narok helps pull them up. They fly away seemingly in the clear. Diterexitre jumps onto Cao and they fly off in a blaze after them. Karok whispers something to his dragon. Just then his dragon turns around and sprays a deadly red and brown flame at Cao. Cao becomes overwhelmed, screeching out, losing control to avoid it. This sends Diterexitre twirling toward the ground.

Descending toward the unforgiving ground Diterexitre passes out, having a flash back from a time very long ago when he was eight-years old. In their old home he watches his father, Loran, from behind a large wooden crate. His father puffs a long pipe, closes his eyes and moans, than opens a black book while beginning to chant indiscreetly. His father has ivory skin, long black hair in a pony- tail, and wears a leather shirt, pants, and boots.

More nervous by the second, Diterexitre, in a time he was innocent, as that little boy, tucks himself further into hiding. Diterexitre sneaks away. He's than walking down a hallway, hearing beautiful music from a stringed instrument. Allured by the sound, he follows it to the next room. He peeks in to the living room, at last finding the sight of his mother, Lopah, named after an ancient root of a tree as rare as a blue moon.

Remarkably so, Lopah passionately plays the instrument. She is dressed similar to his father, yet has pale grey skin. The room is very plain, dusty, and dark. Yet across the room a ray of light does shine. Diterexitre, semi conscious, coming to while lying on the ground, moans to himself.

CHAPTER 39

Trenta Bracing Its Walls

The main square of Trenta has hundreds of tents set up as some people do what they can to go on with the rest of their lives. An enormous banner fashioned sign says, 'Arts and Science Fair'. Thousands of Sabonians, as well as hundreds of Alphinians roam the fair. An inventor, an older Alphinian, who has extremely pale, very light blue skin, wearing tan suede pants and brown shirt, stands in front of a group of children.

In a soothing voice he says, "Inventions of the sailboat, the wagon, the glider, have changed our world." The inventor reaches into his pants pocket and reveals a small clock. The children are in awe at the hands of the clock ticking. A bell ringing from a small guards station in the towns border within the outskirts of the forest alerts them. Most caring, the inventor says, "Go find your families now, all of you."

Hundreds in the fair begin screaming as they see Diterexitre walking in front of an army of soldiers heading toward them. Diterexitre raises his hands in front of him and an oily, jelly like ooze and gas begins to surround the city.

Diterexitre commands, "Take every strong elf!" Dozens of villagers, male, female, varying ages, all begin to panic or scream. A female villager, a Sabonian with light ebon skin, about thirty years old, wearing green suede pants and a brown sweater, sees the sky and land literally becoming black all around, saturated with a plague. She shouts, "It's surrounding us!

While inside one of the homes, several villagers scurry to put out a fire in a fireplace. One of them and the girl's father are hitting the fire with thick rags. Praying for all that they still believe is worth fighting for, and clinging to keep their family alive best they can. A young girl is looking out a window while crying. The girl has gray skin and brown hair. She becomes terrified when she bafflingly seeing Diterexitre up close. She hears screams from outside and sees villagers running, others falling.

The young girl's attention is attracted into the sky, hearing a swooping noise. Curiously, she becomes happier when spotting what spawned the sound derived from, Driona. The Dragon Hawk flies in and out of the clouds. Driona's voice is heard in the young girls mind, "Leave the fire lit if you wish, they won't find you. It's a flame to remind you of hope. One you will find protected by your King and Queen." The young girl smiles and looks away from the window and to her family.

The family looks scared, realizing someone may see the fire they have brewing in the fireplace. The father says, "It won't go out! Hurry their going to see us!" The young girl runs over to the fire- place and says, "It's ok, we are safe, come." She pulls on her father's hand, walking him to the window. They look out the window, seeing Driona for a split second before fading away in the thickness of new clouds forming on the windy night.

Miles upon miles away further north. The others take off, leaving the body of Asate with Barok, standing there with a handful of other Dwelvens in the background on their mountaintop. Karok, Narok, and Sabian, fly away, holding Galtrit and Garbug's bodies.

A short time later in the warm, comfort of the Mountain Dwarves High Chamber, Karok, Narok, and Sabian are sipping from mugs sitting in front of a roaring fire. Sabian has a wet cloth on a cut on his chest. A knock at the door alerts the three of them. Karok responds, "Come!" A dwarven, hooded female cleric comes into the chamber, she reports, "Our clerics our doing all they can, though I believe our scouts, will not me alright. Their essence has been absorbed." Karok lowers his head, the cleric half bows than exits, closing the door behind her.

Narok, "Curse Diterexitre for this." Sabian says softly after a long beat and he himself lowering than slightly lifting his head upward a bit, "How did you know I was there?" "Since you freed me brother from that place we haven't been able to take an eye off of it." Narok replies aggressively.

CHAPTER 40

Three Lost Souls

Montage of Diterexitre, silently killing Wafiroth, Spairo, and Rockerie while they sleep in their chambers. In his astral, gaseous form he goes from one of them to the other, filling his victims with the black ooze. Slipping out into the night as a thing of the elements as a lifeless like nightmare himself. For that is what he has become. Rejected from the very people that he used to have much in common with. Labeled an outcast, perhaps for the last time in history, one would only hope.

CHAPTER 41

The King's Free

Icy mountains, towering to the height of the clouds, are in the far distance at there back- sides. A blue stream runs out underneath, weaving in a unpredictable way through a jungle battling for the privilege of life, so grand by design. One end feeds soft, sandy beach along the coast's ocean shore. Wonderful is the scent of fruit among flowers by the hundreds, safe guarded thus far.

Green and purple palm- trees, gigantic in size, outline the stream, flowing out to the ocean. Sabian, Narok, and Karok are flying on the red dragon over a vast jungle. Sabian, "The other stone doesn't lie, what we seek is here!" A wild array of wild life prospering on a globe being torn at with conflict, held together by the hearts of its most honorable.

Karok is standing at the stream, facing the thick jungle. He looks to the ocean in front of him. Never before have the waves impression upon him as they do. One after the other gives him a satisfied vibe of nature being eternal. In a constant state of evolution. He pulls out a sandstone dagger and slices a vine on a tree. He grabs the branch, holds it upside down, and starts drinking blue juice that start flowing out. He is wearing stone plated armor.

Standing beside Karok is his brother Narok. Karok states a simple, inspiring comment, "Ah the warm air of summer." Narok asks genuinely concerned, "Are you alright brother?" Karok puts one of his hands under a wave crawling up to where he is kneeling on one knee. Reaching down he closes his eyes as he scoops up a handful of sand and seawater. Upon opening them he says this, "I will be." He sighs, straining to a degree to look at his brother standing over his shoulder with the big ball of light that is the sun high up in the sky.

"It was horrible, the screaming, the suffering, it was unimaginable...the burning people alive once he had, had used them up." Narok kneels beside him, "I am sorry brother." A scuffle behind them throws off the moment, "Did you hear something?" Narok asks, assured he heard something from the jungle. "Don't worry, it's probably Sabian." The two pair's of eyes stare into the mysterious, thick jungle.

Both of them stand up, eyes widening in disbelief at the uncanny viewing of hundreds of tiny branches breaking as movement within the shady vegetation occurs. Karok grasps his battle-ax tighter. Narok, "What is it?" Karok, "Not Sabian!" A horde of Klinkis, six inches tall, cute gigantic eyes, with a body of both a porcupine mixed with a reptile more than make themselves visible as they start popping out of the jungle all over the shore, surrounding the two brothers.

Narok, "What are they?!" Karok, "Klinkis'!" Growling is nearly lost a mist the animals hissing. In estimate of two hundred of these Klinkis gather themselves. 2In the sky Sabian is flying Karok's red dragon over the tree-tops. Narok reaches into a small sack that is around his shoulder and pulls out a thin- chained net. He throws it toward a close group of Klinkis. The net unravels fifteen feet in radius, covering a dozen of them and pulling them down to the ground. In an avalanche way all the other creatures rush them. From out of nowhere just than Sabian pulls on the dragon's reigns, descending downward. The dwarves jump on.

Later that evening Diterexitre is sitting in his throne. Cao is in the small form of a dragon elf, standing on her shoulder. Diterexitre widens his eyes and says. "Yes it is time we turn the odds in our favor. In a sphere of pink and light purple hues, Diterexitre hovers, raising his hands over his head, summoning fragments of asteroids floating in far around them in space. Only a moment is needed until he has formed a massive, single piece. With all of his might he chants something indistinguishable to hurl the rock toward the planet, precisely over Hiltovia.

While in front of the Hiltovian castle another battle brews. A legion of Diterexitre's most corrupt in their former lives was sent to the desert lands. Several thousand Hiltovians led by King Valinor fight on. Against soldiers, led by the one named Vilanowa. Vilanowa falls into a state of meditating, semi conscious state, closing his eyes and chanting something indistinct.

Reopening them Vilanowa is first to look up into the sky seeing the asteroid head toward them." Let this be an end to all this conflict." Seconds later a scout in one of the cities tower tops blows a horn, spotting what only appears to be doom headed directly toward them. A platoon of lords and knights round Valinor look up as for an instant the mayhem of the battle ceases as warriors mid strike or stride pause at the site.

Trailing behind the asteroid is a flaming trail. Scurrying past his circle of guards around him Valinor frantically runs from the battle- field. "My King?" One of the lord's shouts after him though is blindly ignored. Running up to the solid gate that the Sabonian Queen could not pass, "Open the gate!" he yells. Under his breath he says, "Ellaina"

Inside the gate his wife and daughter have spotted the asteroid. "Ellaina?!" They run to greet each other, he hugs her and his daughter with his other hand. Thousands of others are screaming terrified, running to loved ones and would be shelter wherever they can. Valinor falls to hysteria, breaking down and falling to his knees, beating himself up for his arrogance, "Forgive me." he says. Ellaina leans down to him, "What do you mean?" A few tears roll down his cheek as he tries to find the right words to say. "I turned down the Sabonian's union, I… A whirling sound encroaches as the asteroid is very close.

His daughter steps right up to him, in a sweet voice says, "Poppa, will you save us?" No more than four years old, adorable in every fathomable way, staring right into Valinor's eyes, as he has a flashback of Sabian's words saying, "Do you want our children to have the same struggles. Valinor opens his mouth, shaking some than just pulls her close to him and hugs her tightly, I am sorry." He says.

Blasting in the air is a series of horns blown by soldiers on the top of the towers, undertone by chaotic shouting. Looking to the horn blowers Ellaina, Valinor, than his daughter spot Sabian flying in fast over the city toward the asteroid. Sabian yells out in a strain that nearly breaks him in two, positioning himself under the asteroid. All anyone could possibly do he pushes against the jagged surface. Teeth clenching while every one of his muscles throbs, stretches, and grows.

Miraculously, with an eye- blinding site for all helplessly staring up in whatever form of pray they believe in Sabian wins momentum. Flooding externally was a roaring red, blue, and white energy of the Magic of the Stars like never before, as it too shot from our very sun and within him. If one could see inside him they would see his heart had to be blessed for his insides were readying to give up though it is his spirit that prevails. Gaining enough distance from the planet, breaking the atmosphere into the stratosphere he gives one final thrust outward, hurling the asteroid out into space.

Nearly passing out, Sabian catches his breath, slowly, triumphantly, descending back throughout the clouds to the surface. "He, he saved us." Valinor whispers, ashamed his prejudices got in the way of his thinking earlier, as well as over the years. Ellaina say's "He has saved us all." Speechless for the most part, besides gasps of disbelief, the crowd of countless thousands of Hiltovians think they are witnessing a god, as he silently lands in front of Valinor.

Valinor says, gaining a at the very least a piece of his pride back "Any who would sacrifice himself and his people has my allegiance, forever, High King." Valinor says to Sabian, who in return nods. Sabian flies off, passing Karok and Narok waiting on their tired dragon atop a nearby mountain- top.

CHAPTER 42

Of Trenta Main Square Fina Stand

Drusaka and Feltak, back to back cutting down soldiers of Diterexitre's. Feltak wields a staff and Drusaka a mace, yet dozens of more soldiers are heading toward them. One soldier swings an ax at her, yet she ducks just in time. Feltak pushes the soldier off of her. Lituluka rides over with a group of a few hundred soldiers, raising his ax to cut the sky.

"Attack!" All several hundred soldiers behind him flood around him and toward the elves. Feltak, "Press onward!" General Draven, a Sabonian with a mix between ivory and gray skin, fairly charasmatic, light bluish green eyes, and battle worn red plate armor, has dozens of knights riding behind him as he charges up to Drusaka and Feltak. Draven, "They've broken through our outer wall's defenses! We need to close the outer gate and make our stand here Feltak!" "Do it General!" Draven grabs a horn around his neck and blows, hundreds of knight's form on him.

Later that evening in Trenta's Hospital a handful of knights stand guard near the door of the chamber. Drusaka, exhausted, looks up to a scout walking over. "My lord, we've managed to push them back outside for now and the others simply disappeared." Each of the warriors are lying on cots, covered in blood, and some of which have limbs missing... moaning, and some screaming, are all around the grounds. "They must be regrouping." Drusaka adds in closing.

In a village home, the young boy, Vi, has a face filled with terror painted on his cute, doll like face. He runs out from behind the woman, and heads to Feltak, her royal robes twinkling in the. The child runs up to her. Feltak kneels down to the boy. The knights patrol further. Feltak, "What's wrong Vi?"

Vi, "I'm scared." Vi's mother walks over, "Come now Vi." Feltak and the woman smirk at each other. Vi hesitates. Feltak, "Well now Vi, that's a brave name, after a Dragon Hawk if I'm not mistaken. Who gave it to you?" The woman says, "Go on Vi, its ok." Olan, "My father…though he passed away.

In a most soothing voice of the somewhat elder Feltak, she says, "For tonight though we've asked all the children of Trenta to send a special pray out before heading to bed." Vi, "All right." Feltak, "Arch Mage's orders Vi. I'm sure as your father is thinking of you, he'll want you to get you're strength, for tomorrow will be another day, a better day." Vi, "Ok, goodnight mam.

Woman, "Thank you." Feltak takes a small dagger out from her belt. Feltak, "If it's all right with your mother…" She nods ok. "Can you hold onto this for me?" Feltak, holding the dagger out in her hand. Vi takes the dagger. Vi, "I'd be honored." Woman, "Thank you." "We will do all we can to make sure you are both safe." Vi and his mother nod than walk to their home and close the door behind them.

Inside their living room Vi and his mother have no idea that the fates are painting a freigtening evening, two of Diterexitre's soldiers are hovering in front of the largest window…scheming with another soldier coming up to the window outside.

Two of the soldiers' head up a staircase while the other is attracted to a lantern hanging on the wall. Vi, in his bedroom and half asleep, half asleep and rubbing his eyes, wears a leather shirt and long cotton pants as he slips on his furry slippers and slowly turns a doorknob. In the hallway Vi whispers, "Mama?"

A lump comes to Vi's throat as he sees the two soldiers drifting down the hallway.

With panic struck eyes he carefully steps back into his room and pins himself against the wooden wall. He looks to his night table, about ten feet away, where a lit candle flares beside the dagger Feltak gave him. Moonlight coming from the one window in the room reflects onto the dagger's shinny long steel blade. He begins to tip toe to the night table when he hears chatter from outside.

Vi looks outside the window and sees Feltak in the center of many guards twenty- feet below him, and pointing to the house. Vi is about to tap on the window when he stops himself and looks around nervously, than turns to the dagger.

He quietly walks to night table, picks up the dagger, and walks back to the window. He begins moving the dagger around, trying to catch the moon's light to reflect it out of the window. He begins to sweat, than catches the light just right and shines it down near Feltak and the others. Feltak notices the light and looks around him. Vi gets excited that Feltak sees him, and drops the dagger on the floor, causing a crash.

While in the hallway the two soldiers are morphing into a black, purple, and pink vapor, passing through a closed door at the end of the hallway when they stop, and morph back to their semi solid form. Their eyes are somewhat life like with an elf's features mixed with a ghost.

Feltak is stunned. She runs toward the front door with every step full with the hope that the family is still alive. Inside Vi's mothers bedroom the soldiers are starring out the window when they hear the door barge open, and sees Vi enter. The mother stirs, than wakes up. The soldier's hovers to Vi. His mother, wearing a flannel shirt and tan pajama bottoms, jumps out of bed and picks up a long sword under from under her bed. Vi, petrified, holds the dagger up high with one hand. The soldier's circle him, growling nastily.

The mother is about to swing at the soldier when she notices their elf like ears than says, "You are like us, aren't you?" The soldier's hesitate, turning from Vi, probing the mother for a long beat. Hovering over much closer to his mother, as their eyes grow wider. Roaring the half beast soldiers scratches her in the chest with his long fingernails. The moon falls behind the clouds outside.

She screams out and falls over, barely keeping her eyes open. Vi dives at the possessed soldier's with the dagger aimed at them yet misses. One of the soldiers scratches Vi on the shoulder, he falls to the floor, holding his bloody shoulder. Vi screams out.

Feltak bursts into the room. She has a few scratches on her neck and hands. A blue fiery shield of light emanates from her entire body encompassing Vi, the woman, and the soldiers. The soldiers scream out and burn away. Feltak grows weary, and just as she falls over the mother and Vi catch her.

In a sphere of pink and light purple hues, Diterexitre hovers above Trenta. His eyes are fixated on the main tower below. In a cloud Lituluka and Drexzulath appears behind him. Stars themselves are affected by the powers they are attuning from dark matter at their disposal.

A threatening army of several thousand soldiers form in rows in the sky behind them, each as possessed with a dark spell festering within. Diterexitre raises his arms as the army disperses throughout the city streets. The knights in the guard towers of the outer and inner walls of the kingdom ring bells now as they see the invaders appear.

Diterexitre's army infiltrates the surrounding area of the hallway, breaking in through the glass windows. Battening down the entryways and in a gang ambush fashion completely overwhelm the guards at their stations. Relentlessly soldiers walk among the aftermath of the battle even hacking away at the wounded.

Diterexitre, Lituluka, and Drexzulath, appear in the large hallway, all fire various forms of dark energy at Alderon, Feltak, Draven, Ban, Karok, Narok, the Dwelven coming out from around the corner. Making every second count the threesome pours the combined might. Lituluka and Drexzulath step beside Diterexitre as countless members of their army appear behind them, filling the hall and petrifying the High Council.

Ban yells out to the others surrounded, "It's a trap!" Diterexitre yells "Charge!" He takes the lead as all the others follow. Lituluka teleports behind Alderon and Feltak and stabs them both through the back. Drexzulath appears behind Draven and Ban and slits both of their necks with a black razor like knives that appear from the thin air. All of the council is battered down and the army disperses through the castle. "Find the King!!!" Diterexitre commands. Within mere moments the High Council falls in domino effect, to their ultimate demise, cut down to the ground by the opposition.

Sabian, Zutsiar, Nikoli, Kulundra, Totec, and Drusaka are below in the Main Square of the city, trapped under a huge pile of rubble. Drusaka, Nikoli too, feel the great loss of the others. "It's almost too much to bear. We have lost many. The time is now or never." Drusaka says, just than, as though on queue, Sabian regains consciousness. "Sabian?" Nikoli. She, as the others, also half out of it, as a thick cloud of debris fills their lungs.

Everyone does what all they can to grab a piece of rubble off of Sabian. "He took the worst of the blow trying to blunt it from us. Together, each of us, reaching into ourselves, touch him, with all the luck and might in the world let it be enough!" Nikoli says, as each of them struggles moving pieces of rubble away. A ship is near to the shore of Trenta's beach coast. On it are some of the finest crewman the world has ever known, accompanying, Uljohn, Willa, and the Black Lion.

Pressured under the dirty rubble coming on them, Nikoli, apparently possessing the sharpest hearing of the group is drawn outside. "Something's stirring outside the rubble!" She shouts, pointing beyond the carnage of their monument around them. The others hear it now too. Zutsiar says, "It may be Diterexitre?"

Nikoli hurls her arms above her head, closing her eyes, throwing up a yellow spherical shield. Straining intensely she is able to peak at Drusaka, as he has been a tutor of sorts. He nods respectably to her than turns his attention to Sabian. Sending chills down their backs they hear Diterexire shout out, "Where are you?!" Remaining silent, the group glances to each other, hoping that he will stride away without another sound. Diterexitre screams out, proceeding to walk toward them. "We have to hurry." Nikoli whispers.

Sabian stirs, reaching out to touch upon the great and mysterious energies from ancient pyramids around the world. The one they have built in their city erupts in various ways of semi transparent energies, as do the others, absorbing the majestic nature of the oceans, trees, earth, and sky. The others around Sabian gather even closer, hearing the chant of Drusaka just above the whooshing of energies stirring outside of their cave of fallen stone.

Through the tiniest of cracks the energy from the pyramids comes whooshing into Sabian himself. With lightning speed Sabian throws up a ray of solid red, blue, and white light. Deflecting all of the debris clear from over his friends and family. Diterexitre summons Drexzulath and Lituluka, along with his army beside him.

Yelling and grunting from his soldiers pierces the air as they filter beside him. Sabian shouts, "Get back!" The others look to him, heeding his words, though still standing near him. Nikoli says, "We are not leaving each others side." Standing firm as could be, despite being battered, Sabian nods to them than stares to Diterexitre, who shouts, "End this Diterexitre!"

Diterexitre heeds not the words of the elven High king. Lashing out in a violent tornado like spell of ebon, purple, and pink energy Diterexitre strives on for the death of those around him. Sabian takes the blunt of the blow, straining greatly to keep his hands up to deflect some of it. The others are in a lot of pain, despite their best efforts, meager spells and hand weapons, can't withstand the brute force of Diterexitre.

Drexzulath and Lituluka fight with Zutsiar, Drusaka, Nikoli, and Kulundra. In the nearby back- ground soldiers fight off knights and villagers when Willa and Uljohn walk onto the scene. Diterexitre continues to pour on the dark magic, now with Sorg as well, appearing by his side to his astonishment. "How is this possible?" By Cao. I have come to your aid!" Diterexitre is about to rebuttal when Willa walks beside Sabian. Willa and Sabian, both of which have just flared up in the Magic of The Stars.

Although Willa and Sabian's magic starts disintegrating the soldiers forces surrounding them, hundreds more appear around them including Drexzulath and Lituluka. Many soldiers close in on Sabian's friends. Sabian desperately tries to concentrate harder, straining harder. "Your friends and family are leaving your side! With every moment!" Sabian confused for a moment, looking to Drusaka than to Nikoli and Zutsiar, shouts back. "What do you mean?" 'Diterexitre steps closer, as Drexzulath, Sorg, and Lituluka come beside him.

"The others." Sabian than looks up and says, realizing somehow Alderon and the others are gone… to the other side. At that moment he realizes whom he has lost, dear friends. With that comes a crane load of remorse. He can barely stand. Diterexitre's magic combines remarkably to everyone's astonishment with the Magic of the Stars. A cataclysmic force of both dark and light magic explosively combine…the ground begins shaking and falling apart as it strikes at every one as once.

Out of nowhere Diterexitre disappears. Every one of the survivors shared a common thought. This very moment was the calm before the final storm. Laughter echoed by the Dark Lord echoed through the city. He and his minions are not far at all. Sabian's suspicious, suddenly from out of the clouds comes Diterexitre, in a eye shocking sight, the others in his company merge into him.

Hundreds of his army all consumed by a rainbow of energy. For an instant Diterexitre's eyes close, and the rainbow enters Cao. Cao forms larger than ever. Diterexitre transforms into a dragon, into the giant Graziloth. A thirteen- headed dragon, lashing out at everyone around, sending them to dive for cover and most to scream out in fear.

Appearing from out of nowhere, together are the spirits of Driona, Feltak, Wafiroth, Spairo, Mar, Rainerie, the Black Lion, Darion, and Holera. Sabian, despite the pain he's in, smiles back. Graziloth lashes out, literally causing Sabian and countless others who are nearby to shriek out. A humming sound that is accompanied by circular shaped rings of electrical discharges comes from Graziloth's body, causing havoc all around.

In screaming out, rooted from the pain of losing his friends, now possibly everything else within the world Sabian flies up in the air to meet the creature eye to eye. The others below look up in fear with a glimmer of hope resonating somewhere within them. Willa, in a blur, flies off beside Sabian as fast as a rocket. Within seconds another stage strikes them as though they are one, with a blue red, and white light coming over their bodies entire. They merge, altering to a pure, living like comet of electricity, with a face hardly recognizable.

Slicing off each and every one of Graziloth's thirteen heads. More rubble falls as the beast's flames strike the castle, yet there is Nikoli standing strong still as the others are not. She throws up a shield, she holds firm, she holds brave. As the aftermath settles Sabian and Willa land.

Willa and Sabian separate back to normal. Uljohn looks her in the eye, feeling so happy inside that all is well. Peace is there reward. Sabian and Nikoli, staggering a bit, walk to meet and share a long hug between them, like there is no tomorrow and no end, after all. "Diterexitre is no where to be found." So says voices near and far from all those survivors gathering. Sabian and the others glance around to what remains of their loved ones and city.

The planet saved, anchored with an ocean of countless stars. Nikoli and Sabian look to each other in the main square of the castle of Trenta. On the first day of summer the air is livelier than ever.

Uljohn walks toward Sabian and Nikoli, holding a book. "My friend, I believe this belongs to you." What is it?" Sabian asks. "A book of your people's origin, washed up on the shores of my city years ago, though a bit faded, I give it to you." Reaching out for it each of them wonders what is intact inside of the thick, worn book. "Thank you my friend." Sabian passes it to Nikoli as she seems quite curious.

She carefully flips through the pages, Sabian and Uljohn over her shoulder peeking. "Hmm I wonder what you have to say." Nikoli says. Sabian and Uljohn smile and nod to each other. In the middle of the book they see an illustration of mountains and a valley. In the center of the valley is a group of elves, some knights, on foot as well as on Dragon Horses. They do not find familiar anyone yet there is a tiny caption above a tall, bald, young male elf with ivory skin, and a beautiful, fierce young elven female with long hair and beige like ivory skin, that says, "The Magic of the Star's children, Prince Priscus and Princess Nichole, forever they stand upholding peace throughout the land."

Nikoli looks away for an instance, "What is this?" She asks looking to both of them really asking her self out loud. "A Prince and a Princess?" She says looking now to Sabian. "Our children perhaps it is the future." Sabian says. Uljohn pats them on the back, "No one has ever heard of them in the past." He smiles to them and walks away. Nikoli and Sabian smile to one another, and hug, look to each other one more time, than hug again. Third time is the charm.

END
Written by Nick Paratore

CPSIA information can be obtained
at www.ICGtesting.com
Printed in the USA
BVHW031755170720
583973BV00001B/111